For the Promise

THE RAIDER BROTHERS

D.E. Haggerty

Chapter 1

*Blossom — a woman who loves adventure — as long
as it fits within her time schedule*

Blossom

I bounce on my toes and rub my hands together. "This is going to be awesome."

Dakota stares up at the rollercoaster. "I don't know."

I elbow her. "The *Siren's Spiral* is meant for children."

"There are over-the-shoulder harnesses."

"Safety is important."

She points to the loop. "It goes upside down."

"Thus, the over-the-shoulder harness."

"Upside down doesn't scream children." She motions to the line. "And there aren't many children waiting."

I bat my eyelashes at her. "Please go on the rollercoaster with me. You'll be my best friend."

She snorts. "You proclaimed me your best friend two minutes after we met."

Of course, I did. Dakota and I are two of the few people who live full-time on the island of Smuggler's Hideaway but didn't grow up here. Everyone else on the island has friends they've known since they were in diapers.

"Best friends go on rollercoasters together."

She shakes her head, but she's smiling. "I guess I have no choice."

"Yea!" I shout before throwing my arms around her. She stiffens in my embrace for a few seconds before relaxing. I don't know Dakota's story yet. But she's obviously been hurt and doesn't trust easily. I haven't pushed her since I understand not trusting easily. And, okay, maybe I don't want to tell my story either.

I release her before pushing her toward the line.

"Twenty minutes from here," Dakota moans as she reads the sign.

I set the alarm on my phone for twenty minutes.

"Did you just set an alarm?"

"Duh. We can't keep on schedule if we don't manage our time properly."

She stares at me. "Manage our time properly? We're at an amusement park on our day off."

"And we have a whole list of attractions to fit in. *Carol Carousel, Atlantis Adventure, Kraken's Drop, Grotto Rapids,* and *Triton's Twister.*"

The *Mermaid Mystical Gardens* amusement park names all of their rides after mythical creatures or places. Which is fitting since the park is located on the spot where a mermaid supposedly dove to her death after her pirate lover died.

"You're crazy if you think I'll go on a ride named *Kraken's Drop*."

I curl my bottom lip in a pout. "And here I thought you were fun."

"And here I thought you knew better than to try and emotionally blackmail your best friend."

I snort. "Ha! What's the purpose of a best friend if you can't emotionally blackmail her?"

"I'm beginning to regret walking into *Pirates Pastries* the day we met."

I throw an arm around her. "Don't lie. No one can regret a pastry from Parker. Besides, I'm the best thing to ever happen to you."

"And so very modest, too."

I shrug as I drop my arm. "What's the point in being modest? It's not as if anyone else is going to toot my horn."

She groans. "Please tell me you're not carrying around a horn you expect me to toot."

I sigh. "No room for a horn in this tiny bag."

We shuffle a few feet forward. "This line is going to take forever," Dakota whines. "This is the first time we've moved since we've been in it."

I check my timer and frown. "We've been in line for two minutes. I don't think their '20 minutes from here'-sign is correct."

"I hate standing in lines. It's such a waste of time."

I agree with her, but I'm keeping my mouth shut. Dakota will use any excuse to not ride the rollercoaster. She's not getting out of this line on my watch. Even if I have to adjust my plan for the day.

"Let's play a game to make the time pass."

"I think we're a little old for 'I spy with my little eye'."

I grin. "How about twenty questions? Smuggler's Hideaway style."

"What's Smuggler's Hideaway style?"

"You know how the island is obsessed with mermaids, smugglers, and moonshine?"

She snorts. "How could I miss it? Do you know how many women at the *Mermaid Motel* are walking around dressed up as mermaids?"

"You must have lots of fun working at the motel."

"Your definition of fun and mine are not the same."

I ignore her grumpy response since I know Dakota is not a grump. She's just tired. "Are you ready to pick a person or thing related to Smuggler's Hideaway?"

We shuffle forward in the line for a few feet but stop again. "Fine. I'll play. It'll take my mind off standing in line."

"It's twenty minutes. What else do you have to do?"

She taps her cheek with her finger. "Hmm… What would I do? Oh yeah, now I remember. Sleep."

A stab of guilt for denying her sleep hits me – Dakota works two full-time jobs and is always exhausted – but I ignore it. I'm not allowing my best friend to work herself into an early grave. She needs to have some fun, too.

I raise an eyebrow. "You're going to sleep standing up?"

"I…" She breaks off to yawn. "Yes, yes, I am."

"Come on," I plead. "Let's play the game."

"Fine." She gives in. "But only because I'm afraid of what you'll write on my face if I fall asleep."

I gasp. "I would never."

"Because you can't fit any markers in your tiny bag."

I scowl. "I don't know why I couldn't bring my backpack into the park."

She giggles. "Probably because it was filled with tiny bottles of liquor."

"Have you seen the prices of beverages at this place? Outrageous. Do you want to ask questions or pick a person or thing first?"

"Ask questions."

I try to come up with a person Dakota will never guess. It's kind of mean thinking of a legend she doesn't know yet, but it's a game. And I'm determined to win. It's possible I may be a little competitive. Okay. Fine. More than a little.

"I'm ready."

Dakota studies me for a few seconds. "Are you real or imaginary?"

"Yes or no questions only."

"Are you imaginary?"

"Kinda."

She glares at me. "If I can only ask yes or no questions, you can only answer with yes or no."

"Fine," I huff. "Yes."

"Are you a mermaid?"

"Obviously, she's a mermaid," some man behind me says. "She has long, beautiful hair."

I try to ignore him, but he pushes his way forward until he's standing next to me in the line. "What's your name, mermaid?"

"Not interested. I'm talking to my friend." I give him my back but he maneuvers himself until he's in front of me.

"No budging in the line." I'm dead serious. Budging in line is a sin. It causes havoc with time management.

"There's no reason to play hard to get. It's mermaid karaoke season. You're a mermaid. I'm a smuggler. Let's get together."

"Mermaid karaoke season has nothing to do with me."

I'm not lying to get rid of him. I'm a resident of Smuggler's Hideaway. I'm not some woman on vacation on the island dressing up as a mermaid and singing karaoke at the *Bootlegger* bar in a bid to catch a smuggler.

I have no interest in catching a man – smuggler or not. Men are sneaky creatures who are not to be trusted. Rage pokes at me as memories of why men are not to be trusted try to push to the forefront of my mind.

I shove them down. It's my day off and I'm spending it with my best friend. This is not the appropriate moment to reflect on what a fool I was.

"Fine. If you want me to chase you, I'll chase you," the man says.

"I do not want you to chase me. I want you to go back to where you were in line and pretend I don't exist."

His gaze rakes over my body. It is not a cursory gaze. It's a slimy 'I bet I know how you look without clothes on'-gaze. My stomach nearly gurgles as revulsion fills me.

"Sorry, doll, but you're impossible to forget."

I roll my eyes. "Go feed your cheesy lines to someone else. I'm not interested."

"You don't have to be a bitch."

I widen my eyes. "I'm being a bitch because I asked you to leave us alone and when you refused, I tell you I'm not interested? Whatever." I give him my back. I'm not wasting my time on him anymore.

"Where were we?" I ask Dakota.

She glares at the man. "Teaching this piece of trash a lesson."

I bark out a laugh. "I knew we were best friends for a reason."

She raises an eyebrow. "A reason other than you're crazy?"

"Crazy is a subjective word."

She shrugs. "If the subjective word fits…"

"I'm not the one who cuddled an otter she didn't know."

"Viking is adorable."

The man's gaze ping-pongs between us. "Both of you are fucking crazy," he grumbles before pushing his way through the line of people and marching away.

"Good riddance." I wave at him and he gives me the finger. "Wow. Someone didn't get the message about this place being for children." I rub my hands together. "Back to our game. I believe you've used up three questions."

"I'd rather hear about why you hate men."

"I don't hate men. Men can be very useful." I waggle my eyebrows.

"But not for anything else?"

I raise my eyebrows. "Are you ready to tell me your back-story?" Her nose wrinkles. "Right back at ya, sister."

My past is too embarrassing for words. I feel my cheeks heat as I remember what a fool I was. Welp. I've learned my lesson. No more falling for men. No more trusting men.

This woman is officially on a no-men diet.

Too bad I've never been any good at sticking to diets.

Chapter 2

Jaxon – a man who wishes he could gag his brothers. Not permanently. He's not a monster. Just for a few hours a day.

JAXON

I lower the thief into the barrel through the bung hole at the top. Once it's been fully submerged, I pull it back up with a sample of whiskey inside. I pour the whiskey into a glass for tasting before setting the thief on the table.

I'm about to pick up the whiskey when there's a stampede. Three of my brothers – Kai, Zane, and Miles – rush into the distillery. Crap.

"Awesome!" Kai shouts. "I made it on time."

Zane snorts. "This is the one time you're not late."

Miles rubs his hands together. "Whiskey tasting is nearly better than surfing."

I scowl at him. Nothing is better than whiskey tasting. Although, as the master distiller for *Buccaneer's Whiskey & Distillery,* I enjoy the entire process of creating whiskey – from mashing to fermentation to distillation to blending to quality control – my favorite part is tasting the whiskey while creating new recipes.

I glare at my younger brothers. "None of you will be tasting whiskey today."

"Why not?" Kai pouts. "I'm the operations manager for the distillery."

Zane raises his hand. "As the marketing manager, it's important I know the product in order to market it."

Miles smirks. "Same. As the sales manager, I have to love the product in order to sell it."

I blow out a breath. This is why I begged my brother, Eli, not to give managerial positions to our younger brothers. My oldest brother ignored me. The whole point of *Buccaneer's Whiskey* is to create a business for our family, he said.

Shoes squeak on the distillery floor before my other older brother, Rhett, comes into view. There are six Raider brothers in total. Five too many if you ask me.

"Good. The voice of reason is here." Unlike my younger brothers, Rhett isn't a goof-off. He's the CFO of the distillery, and he takes his position seriously.

Miles chuckles. "The voice of sexual frustration is more accurate."

"Ah." Kai feigns sympathy. "Is Dakota still giving you the run around?"

Rhett growls. "Dakota is Eli's assistant. We aren't involved."

Zane waggles his eyebrows. "But you want to be."

Rhett pushes him and they start to scuffle.

"Stop!" I shout. "No fighting in my distillery."

"Dude." Miles shakes his head. "It's not your distillery. It's owned by all of the Raider brothers equally."

"Eli is the majority shareholder," Rhett says. "The rest of us have ten percent of ownership each."

"Why does Eli get fifty percent?" Zane asks. "He's never here."

"As if you are?" Miles asks.

"Oh, please." Zane rolls his eyes. "You're on your surfboard more than you're in your office."

"I get the best ideas on my surfboard."

Kai snorts. "The only ideas you get on your surfboard is which woman in a bikini on the beach you're going to seduce."

Miles smirks. "Those are my best ideas."

"Rhett," I urge. "Can you please get rid of everyone? I need to work."

"Your powers of concentration are legendary. They'll leave once you ignore them."

I indicate the whiskey glass on the table. "I'm tasting whiskey from each barrel to determine how the different flavors will work together to create a holiday blend today."

Rhett winces. "Shit. Sorry."

In other words, my brothers aren't going anywhere without tasting some whiskey unless I bribe them. Relief hits me when the door opens. Eli must be here since Dakota won't enter a room with Rhett in it unless she has to. Those two are constantly at each other's throats. It's exhausting.

Eli strolls toward us. He has brackets around his mouth, and his eyes are dull. This is not a man anxious to kick my brothers out of the distillery.

"What's wrong?" Rhett asks.

"I know." Kai practically bounces on his toes. "Someone had a run-in with the woman who hates him."

Eli snarls at Kai. "Paisley doesn't hate me."

Wonderful. Another feud. Eli and Paisley used to be friends in high school. He had the biggest crush on her. But now she hates him. He should let it go. But he won't.

Kai raises an eyebrow. "She didn't say you are always showing off your wealth?"

Eli narrows his eyes. "How do you know? You weren't there."

"Dude," Miles scoffs. "Have you forgotten what it's like living on the island? You've been away from Smuggler's Hideaway too long."

Eli left the island after he graduated from high school and he's hardly returned in the ten plus years since. He was too busy building the business of *Apparoo* into a multi-billion-dollar enterprise.

"I'm here to stay now," Eli says. "The distillery isn't some hobby."

I purse my lips. "Of course, it isn't. I create award winning whiskey."

He raises an eyebrow. "You create?"

"Are you denying that I'm the person creating the whiskey flavors?"

He blows out a breath. "No. Shit. Sorry. I'm just in a foul mood."

Which is why he should let the whole Paisley thing go. Whenever they have a run-in, he returns to work in a foul mood.

"What are you creating today?" he asks.

I motion to our brothers. "Nothing unless you can get them to leave."

"Why don't we all leave?"

My brow furrows. "It's not yet noon."

"Lunch." Eli nods. "Good idea."

"I didn't mention lunch," I argue. "I don't have time for lunch. I need to taste from each of these barrels."

"You don't have any samples."

"I do." I motion to the table where the whiskey glass is waiting. I scowl when I notice the glass is now empty. "Who drank my sample?"

Rhett lifts his hands and steps back. "It wasn't me."

I glare at Miles, Zane, and Kai.

"In our defense," Kai begins.

"We shared the sample," Miles finishes.

I shoo them toward the door. "Go. Have lunch." At least I'll have some peace and quiet while they're gone.

"Brother trip!" Kai, Zane, and Miles shout in unison.

A brother trip is an idea Eli and Rhett developed to make sure the six of us spent time together when we were growing up after our dad abandoned us. Mom was working several jobs and didn't have much time to spend with us as a family. Eli and Rhett stepped up in her absence.

"You can't declare lunch on a workday a brother trip. And you need four brothers to agree it's a brother trip."

Eli and Rhett gaze at each other for a few moments. Those two always could communicate without words. Finally, they nod.

"Brother trip," they say in unison.

"Does no one care about our agreement to expand the distillery?" I ask.

"I care since I'm the one who managed to procure the exclusive deal with the *Velvet Blossom* restaurant chain," Eli says.

"Good. Then, you understand I don't have time for lunch."

"Come on." Kai nudges me toward the door. "It's just lunch."

I push my glasses up my nose. "Do I appear stupid?"

"Nope. You're your usual nerdy self."

"Calling me a nerd is not the insult you think it is."

"Let's go, nerd," Miles says.

"Fine but no one better drink during this lunch and I will be returning to work within an hour."

"Sure, you will." Zane winks.

We pile into Eli's SUV. Unfortunately, it easily fits all six of us despite how tall we each are. We need the room to spread out.

"You know," Miles says as we drive toward Smuggler's Rest – the biggest town on Smuggler's Hideaway. "I feel a prank war coming on."

I fist my hand before I yank the door open to escape. Jumping out of the vehicle while Eli is driving – no matter how slow he's driving since it's summer and the island is full of tourists – is dangerous.

My brothers are the bane of my existence. I don't have time for a stupid prank war. The expansion of the distillery is no joke. Especially since Kai, who is supposed to be the operations manager and therefore handle the bulk of the expansion, thinks working is a construct developed by 'the man' to put him down.

I put on a sigh. "I guess I can postpone the development of the holiday whiskey and concentrate on a prank war with my brothers instead."

"Whoa!" Zane holds up his hands. "You can't postpone the development of the holiday whiskey. You promised to have it ready by Christmas. I've already purchased the magazine placements."

"I can't do everything. I'm only one man."

"Damn," Miles mutters. "No prank war."

We arrive at *Smuggler's Cove* for lunch and I follow my brothers toward the restaurant. Eli captures my wrist to stop me.

"When did you become this devious?"

"Maybe I've always been this devious."

Being devious is a requirement in the Raider household if you're a nerd who wants his quiet time to study. Miles, Zane, and Kai went wild after Dad left and there was no longer an adult male in the house to control them.

I had no interest in chasing girls or pulling pranks in school. I knew with Dad gone, I had to get good grades in order to qualify for a scholarship if I wanted to go to college. And I was determined to attend college.

Thus, devious.

Chapter 3

"There's no reason to be a jerk." ~ Blossom

BLOSSOM

"I'm sorry, Paisley."

My boss frowns at the ruined brewing facilities of *Five Fathoms Brewing.* The result of a hurricane hitting Smuggler's Hideaway. For the most part, the buildings on the island were untouched.

Except for the brewing facilities. Although the restaurant of *Five Fathoms* can be salvaged, the brewing facilities, which are housed in a separate building across the parking lot, are ruined.

As the brewmaster, Paisley is understandably upset. This is a big setback for the growing business. Especially after they just landed a deal with the *Gourmet Corner* grocery chain to supply their stores across the entire US with beer.

Paisely blows out a breath. "It is what it is."

I nudge her. "You don't have to be stoic with me. I get it."

I'm Paisley's assistant. She has her four friends with whom she founded the brewery and has been best friends with since they were in school, causing trouble. But I'm the one who works closely with her every day. I'm the one who sees how much she loves this business of brewing beer.

I get it. I love it, too. I moved to this tiny island to work with her. And, also, to flee my past but now is not the time for my past to rear its ugly head.

"At least we can continue to brew beer since Eli offered you space in his distillery."

She scowls. "He offered the space to the brewery."

I bite my tongue before I laugh at her response. Eli doesn't give a shit about the brewery, but he does care about one very stubborn redhead who brews the beer.

Unfortunately for Eli, Paisley hates him. Or, she says she does at least. I'm already making bets with her friends about how long it'll be before the two are knocking boots.

"We should probably get going or we'll be late." Paisley is nearly as obsessed with time management as me.

She glares at me. "You don't have to look excited."

I can't stop myself from smiling. "Sorry. Not sorry. I've wanted a tour of *Buccaneer's Whiskey* since I arrived on the island but they don't give tours."

"At least there's a bright side to a hurricane destroying the business," she mutters as she opens the car door.

I pretend I don't hear her as we drive out of town. The distillery is located in the middle of the island between the towns of Smuggler's Rest and Rogue's Landing. There's one more town on the island – Pirate's Perch – but it's tiny and doesn't have any businesses.

"What do you need me to do once we arrive?" I ask.

"We need to ensure all of the facilities are available for brewing beer – water supply…"

Paisley doesn't stop listing all the things we need to check on until we arrive at the distillery. It's a good thing I already spent several days researching the situation since I wasn't able to make any notes while I was driving. Although, knowing my boss, she already made a checklist for me.

We step out of the car and the door to the offices of the distillery opens and Eli appears. I have no interest in the billionaire, but it's not hard to admit how handsome he is. Especially wearing a three-piece custom suit.

Paisley scowls at him and I nearly giggle. It's obvious from the flush on her cheeks and the way her breath catches that she's into him.

"Why do you hate him?" I ask.

She ignores my question and marches toward Eli. I scramble to follow her.

"Eli," she grunts in greeting.

He grins and his blue eyes light up. "Paisley." He grumbles her name and I nearly swoon. Whatever's holding my boss back from him must be big.

I wave. "Hi, I'm Blossom. I'm Paisley's assistant."

"Eli Raider," he introduces himself as if everyone on the island doesn't already know his name.

He's a billionaire on a small island where the inhabitants think gossiping is a sport. Everyone knows every move he makes. Including me.

When silence falls, I rush to fill it. "I'm excited to tour your distillery facilities. I tried to get a private tour, but the master distiller apparently forbids heathens in his distillery."

Eli grins. "My brother, Jaxon, is the master distiller. He's very serious about his whiskey." He motions toward the large garage doors. "Shall we?"

I trail behind Eli and Paisley as we walk toward the doors. Paisley slows down in an effort to lag behind Eli but he slows down along with her. It's hilarious to watch. It's as if they're both dancing but listening to different music.

Eli opens the door with a remote. The door slides open and the distillery is revealed. There's a large empty area where the brewing facilities will be housed while *Five Fathoms* rebuilds. On the other side are barrels and kettles and various other equipment to support the distillery.

I step closer but a man marching toward us has me stopping. I don't want to overstep my bounds. Especially since I'll be working here with Paisley for the next while.

I study the man as he approaches. Unlike Eli, he's dressed in jeans and a t-shirt. He's tall and the t-shirt strains across his chest. He has a bit of scruff on his jaw but I get the feeling he's not trying to look cool or hip. He's also wearing a pair of black framed glasses that scream nerd.

The text of his t-shirt – it says *that's the spirit* with an image of a barrel of whiskey below it – confirms he's a nerd.

If this is what 'nerd' looks like, I'm officially a nerd lover because this man is a tall drink of sexy with a side of handsome.

"A word," he demands of Eli.

"Paisley, Blossom, this is my brother, Jaxon. He's the master distiller," Eli introduces.

Paisley offers him a hand but he spins on his heel and marches away without shaking it.

"Sorry." Eli excuses himself before following his brother.

"Rude," I mutter as they enter a room and shut the door behind them.

Jaxon may be a sexy nerd but he's also rude. It's a good thing I'm off men because I can't stand rude men.

"Shall we get to work on the checklist?" Paisley forms her words as a question, but she's not asking. She hands me a printout. Told you she made a checklist. "You can handle the first page. I'll handle the rest."

I barely have a chance to say *okay* before she's off. I peruse the list and my nose wrinkles. I can't check these items off myself. I need help. I'd love to go into the office and ask Dakota but she doesn't know much about the distillery. Her job is working for Eli directly as his assistant and not for the distillery itself.

I wait a few minutes, but when Eli and Jaxon don't return, I decide to join them. I don't make it to the room where they're holed up before I can hear their voices.

"I don't want them here," Jaxon grumbles.

"Too bad," Eli says.

"It should be a decision for the board, not a unilateral decision made by you."

"This is the decision of the board."

"I didn't vote for it."

"Jaxon," Eli growls. "Don't you want to help out your fellow smugglers?"

"Can't you just give them money or something? You're a billionaire after all."

"This is the best way to help their business."

"But they'll be in my way. In my distillery every day."

I've had enough. I throw the door open and stomp inside. "I don't know what your problem is with us. We don't have cooties."

Jaxon pushes his glasses up his nose. "I didn't say you did."

"And yet you don't want us here."

"It's not personal."

"Feels pretty personal from where I'm standing."

Jaxon frowns. "What does where you're standing have to do with anything?"

Is he for real? Judging by the confusion in his startling blue eyes, he is. "I didn't mean literally where I'm standing. I meant from my perspective."

"Why didn't you say from your perspective then?"

"It's a saying. You know what a saying is, don't you? A maxim, a proverb, an idiom, a—"

He cuts me off with a growl. "I'm not stupid."

I lift my palms in the air. "I didn't say you were." I drop my hands and fist them on my hips. "But I did say your unwillingness to share your distillery with us feels personal."

Eli crosses his arms over his chest. "Believe me. It's not personal. Jaxon doesn't want anyone in his distillery. Not even me and I own half of the company."

"Oh." My anger deflates. "Do you want us to figure out another solution? Paisley is already hurting since her precious brewery was destroyed. I hate to hurt her more."

Sympathy lights up Eli's blue eyes. He obviously cares for Paisley. She may claim to hate him, but she doesn't stand a chance against those eyes.

Jaxon groans, and I glance over at him. He removes his glasses to clean them with his t-shirt. Damn. His blue eyes are even more startling without glasses obscuring them.

My stomach tingles with interest. I remind my body what a jerk he was when we arrived. It doesn't care. It wants to watch those blue eyes flare with passion before his tongue swoops into my mouth.

"I'll adjust to the situation," Jaxon claims before charging out of the room.

I can't help but notice how his jeans cling to his backside. My body nearly demands I follow him. I ignore my body. It's obviously forgotten what happened the last time I got involved with a man.

But I haven't. And I'm not likely to anytime soon.

Chapter 4

JAXON

I slowly pour the whiskey into the glass and set the rest of the whiskey to the side before picking up the next whiskey I've selected for this blend based on its flavor profile. I'm trying to create a slightly smokier flavor for this blended whiskey.

I carefully measure the amount of whiskey I want to add before pouring it into the glass. I swirl the mixture together and—

Whack!

I nearly drop the glass at the unexpected sound. I check the time. It's barely eight a.m. There's no way Kai has arrived at the distillery yet.

I frown as I set the glass down. I hate disruptions, but I'd better check what's going on.

I step outside my office into the distillery and scowl when I notice the garage doors are open and materials are piled high in the empty space we were planning to use for expanding production. Eli stands to the side with his arms crossed over his chest.

"What's going on?" I ask when I reach him.

"I'm solving your problem."

I blink. What is he talking about? "My problem?"

"You're worried about people running around your distillery."

I remove my glasses to massage the bridge of my nose. "There are currently several people running around my distillery. I don't understand how this is solving my problem." I narrow my gaze at him. "This isn't some kind of exposure therapy, is it?"

"Exposure therapy?"

"Don't act innocent with me. You made Kai jump off the cliffs at *Mermaid Mystical Gardens* to 'cure' him of his fear of heights."

Eli snorts. "Kai wasn't afraid of heights. He didn't want to jump from the diving board because he had an irrational fear of losing his swimming trunks in front of the girls in his class."

"He did lose his swimming trunks when he jumped off the cliffs."

He shrugs. "And now he knows there's nothing to be afraid of."

"Except Zane and Miles stole his clothes and he had to hitchhike home naked."

"If I recall, he wasn't afraid. In fact, didn't he end up dating the woman who picked him up?"

I scowl. "We're getting off track here. Why are there people in my distillery? And why are they unloading building supplies?"

"They're building a wall to separate the distillery from the brewery."

"You're building a wall in my distillery and didn't tell me?"

Eli grunts. "It's not *your* distillery."

I lift an eyebrow. Not my distillery? He must be joking. I'm the master distiller of *Buccaneer's Whiskey & Distillery*. If it weren't for me, there wouldn't be any whiskey.

He squeezes my shoulder. "I know you're the distiller and this is your work area, but the distillery belongs to all of the Raider brothers. We work together to make *Buccaneer's Whiskey* a success."

"Which is why the operations manager is here this morning to oversee this project."

"The construction isn't Kai's responsibility. It's mine."

"It should be his. He's in charge of logistics and supplies."

Eli holds up a hand. "I'm not having this argument with you again. I'm handling the construction. We'll be finished in a day."

Because tomorrow Paisley arrives to set up the *Five Fathoms* brewing facilities.

"I expect you to be nice to her."

My brow furrows. "I'm not a mean person."

He chuckles. "You weren't exactly welcoming when she and her assistant were here last week."

"You didn't warn me they were coming. You told me they were here and rushed off to greet them. I don't enjoy being surprised."

He studies me for a moment before giving in. "You're right. I should have kept you informed."

Someone hollers his name and he rushes off. I contemplate the situation for a moment. I don't want the brewery here. I don't want people I don't know running around the distillery. It's why I don't give tours.

But I'm not stupid. I'm well aware there's no way I can change Eli's mind. He's determined to help Paisley even though she obviously hates him. Those two are on a collision course. They better not collide near any of my precious whiskey.

Since there's nothing I can do here, I return to my office.

~~~

When I walk into the breakroom the next day, practically every surface is covered with food. I scowl.

This breakroom is not the one in the offices, which anyone at the distillery can use. It doesn't have Baccarat crystal or a refrigerator full of the fancy water Eli prefers. This is supposed to be the breakroom for the people who are working in the distillery every day – the two distillery assistants, the cellar worker, the cleaning and maintenance person, and the packing and bottling team.

The door flies open behind me and the smell of cherries hits me before Blossom comes into view. Her blonde hair is piled up on top of her head but a few strands have escaped and are clinging to her forehead. I can't help but wonder how her hair would feel if I sifted a hand through it.

The collar of her t-shirt falls off her shoulder, revealing a pink bra strap. She's wearing a pair of shorts showcasing her long, tan legs. I bet those legs would feel fantastic wrapped around my waist while I pound into her.

I frown. I don't wonder how soft a woman's hair is. My cock doesn't twitch at the sight of a woman's long tan legs.

"What's wrong, nerd boy?"

I scowl at her. "Nerd boy?"

She indicates my t-shirt with a flick of her hand. "If you don't want to be called nerd boy, you probably shouldn't wear a t-shirt declaring you're a proud nerd."

I glance down at my t-shirt. I'd forgotten I'd worn this one today. "Oh."

She giggles and happiness lights up her face while her light brown eyes sparkle. Add in her high cheekbones and there's no denying Blossom is beautiful.

"And?" She drums her fingers over the table. "Why are you scowling at the food? Do you believe workers shouldn't be fed? Are you one of those weirdos who follows a longevity diet and sticks to 600 calories a day?" She grimaces. "No, thanks. I'd rather die early with the taste of chocolate on my lips."

"I do not follow a longevity diet. And I have no problem with workers being fed."

"Is it the food itself you have an issue with? Do you avoid cheese? I'm sorry to say this but I don't think we can be friends if you don't eat cheese. Cheese is nearly as heavenly as chocolate."

"I eat cheese."

She throws her arms in the air. "I give up! Why are you scowling at the food?"

I purse my lips. "I wasn't scowling at the food."

She points to my face. "You're still doing it now. What did the food do to you?"

Zane and Miles rush into the room.

"I heard there was food." Miles grabs a plate and piles it high with sandwiches.

Blossom snatches the plate from him. "The food is for the people helping with setting up the brewery. Your hair is wet, and you're wearing board shorts. You haven't been helping."

"He's been surfing," Zane says as he grabs a plate.

"And where have you been?" Blossom asks him.

Zane winks at her. "I'm the marketing guru."

Miles waggles his eyebrows. "And I'm the sales guru."

My stomach sours as they flirt with her. Women always fall at the feet of my younger brothers. I shut down those thoughts. Why do I care if this particular woman falls at their feet? Blossom means nothing to me.

Yes, she's beautiful and sexy. But she's nothing to me. I have no reason to be jealous.

Blossom starts a slow clap at my brothers. "Wow. You must be very proud of yourselves." She nabs the plate from Zane's hands before steering him and Miles toward the door. "This food is not for office workers."

"But—" Miles protests but she continues on as if he didn't speak.

"I have carefully calculated the amount of food based upon the number of people helping. We don't have extra."

She shuts the door behind them. "Men," she mutters.

I hold up my hands. "I promise not to eat any of this food."

"You're fine. I included all of the distillery workers in my calculations."

"And I'm supposed to be the nerd."

She barks out a laugh. "Did you make a joke? All I need to do is prove I don't have cooties and we can be friends."

"Cooties don't exist."

She narrows her eyes on me. "Are you certain?"

"Yes, I…" I trail off when I notice the gleam in her eyes. She's making fun of me.

"I'm teasing you." Her phone beeps with a message and she digs it out of her back pocket. She reads the message and sighs. "No time for lunch for me."

She starts for the door, but I have the weirdest urge to feed her. To take care of her. Before I can question myself, I grab a protein bar and water.

"Here." I shove the items in her hands. "The sound of your stomach rumbling is distracting me."

She smiles and those light brown eyes snare me. I want to step closer to her. I want to watch those eyes flare with passion as I suck on her lips. My cock twitches in agreement.

I step back before I listen to my body and reach for her. Office romances are a bad idea. As evidenced by Eli and Paisley, as well as Rhett and Dakota. None of those couples have gotten together yet, but their mating rituals are causing disruption.

A large object falls to the floor outside the breakroom. Entirely too much disruption.

Chapter 5

"Gotta love when a nerd surprises you." ~ Blossom

A FEW WEEKS LATER

Blossom

I check the time on my computer – one minute past noon – and push away from my desk. Time for some much-needed lunch.

The past weeks have been extremely busy. Setting up a new brewery and starting to brew in record time, since the hurricane destroyed the original facilities, has been exhausting. But also exhilarating. I doubt anyone besides Paisley could have managed it. Of course, she had an extraordinary assistant – aka me – to help her.

I pause as I pass my boss's office. I usually warn her when I go to lunch but since her and Eli have been getting hot and heavy in her office, I'm reluctant to knock on her door. I'm not a voyeur! They think no one knows what they're doing. Spoiler alert – everyone knows.

I whip out my phone and message Paisley instead. I nearly jump when she replies immediately.

Have a long lunch. You deserve it.

I deserve it? Or she wants some privacy to play with Eli? I start typing my question but you know what? I don't want to know. Paisley deserves to have some fun. Especially with a sexy billionaire who follows her around like a puppy dog.

And I have the perfect way to pass the time. I nearly skip as I make my way to Jaxon's office. I've been dying for a tour of the distillery and who better to give me a tour than the sexy master distiller?

I pass the operations manager's office. The door is open, and I check inside, but Kai is nowhere to be found. From what I've learned over the past weeks, this is normal. He's the youngest Raider brother and isn't exactly fond of responsibility.

Must be nice to have an older brother who founded a company to give you a job. I rub a hand over my chest as the familiar pang of loneliness hits. I had the best family ever but no longer. They're gone.

My eyes itch but I inhale a deep breath and push all my feelings away. I'm not having a breakdown at work. Breakdowns are for when you're home alone and have a dozen or two of cookies to help you eat your feelings.

The door next to Kai's opens, and Jaxon walks out.

"Just the man I'm looking for."

Jaxon glances around as if searching for whoever I'm referring to. When he realizes we're alone, he taps his chest. "Do you mean me?"

He's adorable when he's confused. "Yes, you."

Those ocean blue eyes, all of the Raider brothers share, cloud with confusion. "Why are you looking for me? Is something wrong? Has the brewing caused a problem for the distillery? I told Eli this wasn't a good idea."

I hold up a palm. "Slow down, Mr. Doomsday. There's no problem."

His nose wrinkles. "Why are you searching for me if there's no problem?"

I widen my eyes and give him my best innocent look. Judging by how his eyes narrow, I'm not convincing him. "I've tried getting a tour of the distillery many times, but I was told you don't give tours."

"Correct."

I bite my bottom lip. "Maybe you could give me a tour now? Since we're colleagues and all."

He frowns. "I don't have time to give you a tour."

"It's lunchtime. Don't you need a break?"

"I don't have time for a break."

"You need to have a break, even if you're busy. It's important to give your body and brain a pause. It helps boost creativity, increases productivity, reduces stress, prevents burnout, and improves concentration when you return to work."

He studies his watch for several moments. "I have ten minutes before I need to return to my office."

I bounce on my toes. "Thank you! You won't regret this."

"I'm already regretting this," he mutters.

I elbow him. "I'll bring you cookies from *Pirates Pastries* as a thank you. No one can resist Parker's cookies."

"I want a shipwreck cookie."

"That's the spirit."

He motions me forward. "How much do you know about distilling whiskey?"

"I know the basics. Select the proper grains. Grind the grains to grist. Mix with hot water in the mash tun to extract sugars, creating wort. Move the wort to fermentation tanks. Add yeast to turn the sugar to alcohol. At the end of fermentation, you have created wash."

Jaxon holds up his hand to stop me.

"I wasn't finished."

"Why do you want a tour when you know more about distilling whiskey than my brother Kai?"

I roll my eyes. "Kai is the operations manager. He knows how whiskey is created."

"Kai is a goofball who thinks time is a construct created by the 'man' to put him down."

I rear back. "Kai doesn't believe in time management? Does he not understand how important time management is? How do you finish your work on time? Get your product ready to deliver on time? Meet your obligations?"

"Calm down. You're going to make yourself hyperventilate."

I glare at Jaxon. "Don't you dare tell me to calm down. I'll hyperventilate if I want to."

He lifts a brow. "You'll hyperventilate if you want to?"

"Fine. I won't hyperventilate. But you should never tell a woman to calm down."

"Even if she's spiraling out of control?"

"Especially then."

He shakes his head. "I'll never understand women."

"And I'll never understand men."

His brow wrinkles. "Men aren't difficult to understand."

I snort. "You've got to be kidding."

"I don't kid."

I can believe it. Jaxon Raider is a serious man. A serious nerd. And a serious hottie. The confusion on his face is adorable.

The door flies open behind him and Kai rushes inside. He waves as he runs past us.

"No running in the distillery!" Jaxon hollers after him.

"No time. In a hurry!" Kai shouts without slowing.

"Where are you going? We have a safety inspection next week. You're supposed to ensure we're ready."

"We'll be ready!"

I scowl as Kai grabs his bag from his office and runs out of the distillery.

"Must be nice to have job security," I mutter.

"Job security? Are you worried about losing your job? As far as I can tell, Paisley is happy with your performance."

"I'm not worried about losing my job."

"What did you mean then?"

I open my mouth to berate Jaxon. It's obvious what I meant. But his eyes are clouded in confusion. He isn't being deliberately obtuse. He honestly doesn't understand what I meant.

I blow out a breath. "I shouldn't have said anything."

"But you did."

"Can we pretend I didn't?"

He fiddles with his glasses. "I don't enjoy pretending."

I giggle. Of course, he doesn't.

"I'm serious. What did you mean?"

I give in and explain, "Eli founded this company to provide you and the rest of your brothers with jobs. Kai doesn't have to worry about getting fired since Eli would never fire him."

My chest squeezes. How would it feel to have a big brother to care for you? Who worried about you? Who took care of you? I wish I knew.

Jaxon steps closer. "And this makes you sad."

I clear my throat. "I'm not sad."

"The sparkle in your eyes disappeared, and your voice went flat."

My eyebrows fly up. "You don't understand subtlety, but you can recognize sadness?"

"Why are you sad?"

I glance away. "Can we not discuss this?"

He pinches my chin and forces me to meet his gaze. "I don't enjoy seeing you sad."

He doesn't enjoy seeing me sad? My bottom lip trembles. No one's cared about my feelings in such a long time. I forgot how it feels.

His gaze dips to my lips and his eyes heat. "Don't cry, Blossom."

"I..." My words trail off when his lips meet mine. I gasp in surprise and his tongue swoops into my mouth. I moan as the taste of whiskey and mint hits me. It's not a combination I would ever put together, but it works for him.

Jaxon growls before wrapping his arms around me and shoving me against the wall. I can feel every inch of his hard body pressing against me. He feels strong and steady. As if nothing could rattle him.

I wind my arms around his waist and now I'm surrounded by all things Jaxon. His tongue explores my mouth and his hard length presses against my stomach. I massage his ass cheeks and he groans before grinding his cock against me. My panties dampen in response.

Holy mermaids. I've missed this. I've missed being intimate with a man.

I've avoided being intimate with a man because men are not to be trusted. But I don't need to trust this man. I can have fun and keep my heart encased behind a steel wall he can't destroy or climb over.

His hands graze my sides and my nipples pebble in return. Oh yeah. I definitely want to have fun with this man. Lots of naked, sweaty fun until we exhaust each other and go our separate ways.

"Ahem. AHEM!"

The sound of someone clearing their throat manages to break through my sex cloud. Jaxon rips his mouth from mine.

I glance over his shoulder. Paisley raises her eyebrow at us and he steps away from me.

"I need to…" He rushes off without completing his sentence.

Go ahead and run, Jaxon. I do enjoy a good chase.

Chapter 6

JAXON

I pour the whiskey into the measuring cup. The color reminds me of Blossom's eyes. How the color changes based on her mood. How her eyes lightened to a deep gold when she was sad.

The sight of Blossom – the woman who's always laughing and joking – close to tears nearly brought me to my knees. I couldn't stand to witness this vibrant woman shrouded in sadness.

So, I threw caution to the wind and sipped on those pretty pink lips I've been dying to taste since she told me she doesn't have cooties. When her eyes darkened to a brown sherry color as her passion ignited, I couldn't stop myself from thrusting my tongue into her mouth to explore.

She tasted of temptation itself, sweet and fiery, causing a rush of warmth to spread to every part of me. It was better than any whiskey I'd ever distilled. My cock hardens at the memory.

My hand feels wet. Shit! I've spilled the whiskey all over myself while I was reminiscing about a simple kiss.

It wasn't a simple kiss.

I try to argue with myself but I don't lie. There was nothing simple about kissing Blossom. I was ready to rip her clothes off and have my way with her against the wall. The wall in my distillery. Where I should be working.

I've never felt such a powerful attraction to any woman before. Not even in my teenage years when I first discovered sex. I scowl. I don't enjoy not being in control of my emotions.

This won't do. I can't allow myself to be distracted. *Buccaneer's Whiskey & Distillery* will fail if I don't give it one hundred percent of my attention.

I dump the whiskey and clean my station. I'm washing my hands when someone knocks on my door. I ignore it. I've been distracted enough this morning.

The door opens, and Blossom skips into my office.

I scowl at her. "Why did you knock if you're going to barge inside anyway?"

She rolls her eyes. "I figured you were concentrating on your whiskey and didn't hear me."

"And you decided to disturb me?"

She shakes a *Pirates Pastries* bag at me. "Don't you want your cookie?"

"Cookie?"

"I promised you a cookie if you gave me a tour of the distillery yesterday."

A tour we never started because we were too caught up in kissing each other. My cock twitches at the memory. It wants me to kiss her again. Lay her down on my table and taste every inch of her skin. Does it taste of cherries the same way she smells of them?

I ignore my cock. It has a mind of its own when it comes to Blossom. But I'm not allowing a woman to distract me.

"We didn't do the tour."

She smirks. "I know."

"I don't deserve a cookie if we didn't do the tour."

She bites her bottom lip. "Trust me. You deserve this cookie."

Her provocative tone has my cock hardening and lengthening in my jeans. It's ready to accept what she's offering. She sashays toward me, but I hold up a hand to stop her.

"I'm busy. I need to get back to work."

"You can't take a break?" She bats her eyelashes at me.

I fist my hands before I reach for her and draw her into my arms. It would be so easy. But if I can ignore my brothers setting off rockets in the living room while I'm studying for a physics exam, I can ignore this tempting woman standing in front of me.

"Not now."

She bites her bottom lip. "But maybe later?"

"I'm extremely busy."

"You have to take a break sometime," she sings before skipping out of my office.

As soon as the door closes behind her, I release the breath I was holding. Blossom is entirely too tempting. Her presence plays havoc on my emotions. This won't do.

I can't afford any distractions, especially confusing emotional ones. I should avoid her. I nod. Good idea. I'll avoid her and any distracting emotions I don't have time for.

My stomach grumbles some time later and I check the time. It's past two. Lunch has come and gone and I didn't realize it. I make a few notes regarding where I am in the blending process before making my way to the break room.

I grab a yogurt, an apple, and some water. I'll eat these in my office while I type up my notes.

"Aha! Found you!" Blossom hollers and I nearly drop my food.

"Um," I mutter as I fumble with the containers.

"I hadn't noticed your t-shirt before. It's cute."

T-shirt? Why is she talking about my t-shirt?

"Technically, the glass is always full. With air and water." She giggles. "True."

"Um." I inch backwards until my back hits the wall. The door is too far away. I have to pass Blossom to escape.

"Are you trying to make yourself invisible?"

I don't answer since making myself invisible is exactly what I'm trying to do, but it sounds silly when you actually speak the words out loud. I'm not a silly person. I'm a serious person.

"You do realize I can see you?"

I slam my eyes shut as embarrassment fills me. Social situations make me nervous enough but what am I supposed to do when I'm trying to avoid a person but she won't let me? I have no experience with this.

"I can still see you even though your eyes are closed."

Someone – anyone – interrupt us. I've never wanted one of my brothers to arrive and be annoying more than in this moment. Usually, I want to throw them in the ocean and dare them to swim to Europe. None of my brothers can resist a dare.

"Are you afraid of me?"

My body shivers at the close proximity of Blossom. I cling to the items in my hands despite wanting to drop them on the floor in order to touch her.

This is utterly ridiculous. I shouldn't long to touch a woman I barely know. An outgoing, loud woman who is the complete opposite of my quiet persona. A woman who tempts and distracts me.

"What are you afraid I'll do?" she whispers into my ear and I shiver at the feel of her breath touching my skin. "You didn't seem afraid when you kissed me. When your tongue delved into my mouth to taste every inch of me. When you pressed me against the wall and shoved your hardness against me."

My cock is hard and heavy. It wants to accept Blossom's offer. It doesn't understand. I can't be distracted. I don't have the time for an office fling.

And office flings are stupid anyway. When it ends – and it will since this woman could never be interested in boring me for very long – it'll be awkward. And awkward is another distraction I can't afford.

"Fine!" Blossom steps away. "I'm giving up."

Relief hits me.

"For now."

"What's going on?" Kai asks and I open my eyes. He glances between Blossom and me with his brow furrowed.

I hold up my food. "I was grabbing some lunch."

"Lunch? Dude. It's past lunchtime."

"I thought time was a construct devised by modern society to put the man down," I say as I inch toward the door.

Blossom's head rears back. "Time is not a construct devised by modern society."

"Really," Kai drawls. "Why are there clocks everywhere if society isn't trying to shape me into a time following sheep?"

"Time wasn't devised by modern society," Blossom argues. "Calendars and thus time have been around for over 4000 years. Maybe even before then, if you consider many ancient historians believe the tally marks in Upper Paleolithic cave paintings represent lunar months."

Kai's jaw drops open as he stares at Blossom. "You're one of them."

"One of whom?"

"One of the people trying to keep man down with the construct of time."

I nearly chuckle at the disgust on Blossom's face. "Time management is essential to running a business. How do you manage to get all your tasks done if you don't manage your time properly?" When Kai goes to answer, she throws up a hand to stop him. "You know what? Never mind. I don't want to know."

She storms toward the door where I'm lurking and I rush down the hall before she catches sight of me. I make it to my office and slam the door shut behind me. For good measure, I lock it.

The last thing I need is for Blossom to barge inside my office again. She's entirely too distracting. I don't want or need any distractions. What I want is to figure out the recipe for this new blended whiskey. I don't need anything else.

Chapter 7

" I'm making a tactical withdrawal. It's not the same as giving up." ~ Blossom

A MONTH LATER

Blossom

"Why are we doing this again?" I ask Dakota as we fit a sheet over a bed at the *Mermaid Motel*.

"I don't know why you are doing this. But I'm doing this because housekeeping is short-staffed."

We finish making the bed before I have the guts to say the next part. "But you're dating a millionaire now. Surely, you don't need two jobs anymore."

To no one's surprise, Rhett wore down Dakota's resistance to him and the two are now a couple. A solid, sweet couple I'm not envious of at all. Nope. Been down that road and was launched off the cliff when the road ended without warning.

She sighs. "You remind me of Rhett. Quit your job, Dakota. I'll take care of you."

I giggle. "Your imitation of Rhett is horrible."

She blows me a raspberry. "Probably because I'm not a controlling man."

"You love that man."

She sighs and I swear cartoon hearts appear in her eyes. "I do."

"Have you told him you love him?"

Her nose curls up. "Why would I do a foolish thing like that?"

I don't question her further. Dakota's former husband screwed her over bad when he died. I can't blame her for being reluctant to share her feelings.

I glance around the hotel room. "What next?"

She consults her phone. "New water glasses and towels."

I open the door to grab our supplies and nearly run smack dab into Sadie, the manager of the motel.

"I found more cleaning staff. Jada wasn't answering her phone because it's her day off *and* she went to the *Bootlegger* last night and met a sexy pirate. Her words, not mine. They proceeded to drink entirely too many moonshine shots before being kicked out of the bar for trying to sing a duet." She shakes her head. "Everyone knows Mermaid karaoke is for single women only."

"In other words, we're done," I summarize. You never can tell with Sadie.

"Yep. You can go. We're covered. Thanks for coming in. Especially you, Dakota. After working until six this morning."

Dakota flicks her hand. "It was no trouble. I got five hours of sleep before you came pounding on my door."

Sadie grimaces. "Sorry. I may have panicked."

I snort. "May have?"

She pushes me toward the door and into the breezeway. "Go on. Get out of here. Go follow your mermaid dreams."

"I don't have any mermaid dreams."

She plants her hands on her hips. "No dreams about a certain nerdy Raider?"

I scowl. "I'm done with Jaxon."

She rubs her hands together. "Do tell."

I flick my hair. "There's nothing to tell."

Except he kissed me like he needed me more than his next breath before retreating the next day. And in the month since, he hasn't responded to any of my overtures.

Dakota winds her arm through mine and drags me down the breezeway. "There's more to the story."

"Why are you leaving me hanging?" Sadie hollers after us.

"Because you're the biggest gossip on the island," Dakota yells back at her.

"And this is bad because?"

Dakota stops and whirls around to confront Sadie. "Do you want to explain why you practically pee yourself in excitement whenever you get a letter?"

"I don't pee myself. I have excellent bladder control."

Dakota huffs. "Do you want to explain your excitement over your letters?"

"No," Sadie grunts.

"There will be no more gossip about our love lives until you reciprocate."

"You're boring," Sadie pouts.

A woman with long black hair stumbles down the breeze-way toward us. "I'm here."

Sadie grins. "You can tell me all about your night while you clean," she says as she nudges the woman toward the motel room.

"Phew." Dakota runs the back of her hand over her brow. "You're lucky Jada showed up. Sadie is seriously the biggest eavesdropper on the island."

"I reflect that comment!" Sadie shouts from inside the motel room.

I giggle. "She apparently also has excellent hearing."

"Don't I know it," Dakota mutters as we arrive at the elevators.

"Now." I rub my hands together. "What are we going to do with the rest of your day off? Rollercoasters at *Mermaid Mystical Gardens*? Drinks at *Bootlegger* or *Rumrunner*? Lunch at *Smuggler's Cove*? Miniature golf at *Mermaid Mini Golf*? Horse riding at *Sirens & Stables*? Visiting the animals at *Barnacles & Barnyards*?"

She sighs. "I'm exhausted listening to the options, and there isn't even a festival this weekend."

I study my friend for a moment. I should probably let her get some sleep. Working two full-time jobs is exhausting. Especially since her job as the personal assistant for a billionaire is more than full-time.

"If you want to get some sleep, I'll understand."

We walk outside the motel and stand in the sunshine. "I don't want sleep. I want to know why you went from chasing Jaxon to avoiding him."

I scowl. "I don't want to discuss it."

She barks out a laugh. "Too bad."

I cross my arms over my chest and stick out my bottom lip in a pout. "I don't pressure you to tell me everything you and Rhett get up to."

"Because you work in the same building as me and get all the gossip from his brothers."

"Not all his brothers," I mutter.

"What do you want to do today?"

"Go horseback riding at *Sirens & Saddles.* I've never been horseback riding before, but it's on my bucket list."

"I'll make you a deal. I'll go horseback riding with you if you tell me what's going on with you and Jaxon."

I snort. "There's nothing going on."

"I amend my previous deal. I'll go horseback riding with you if you tell me why there's nothing going on with you and Jaxon."

I open my mouth to say because Jaxon is a scaredy cat who doesn't realize what he's missing but she holds up her hand before I can speak.

"*And* you have to be truthful about whether you want him or not."

I glare at her. "You drive a hard bargain."

"I work for a billionaire, and I'm dating a control freak. What do you expect?"

I hold out my hand. "You have a deal, but horseback riding better be awesome."

"There are horses. Of course, it'll be awesome."

"You and your obsession with animals," I mutter as we get situated in my car. I drive toward *Sirens & Saddles*, which is on the other side of the island near Pirate's Perch.

"Out with it. Why have you gone from chasing Jaxon to avoiding him?" Dakota asks before we're out of the parking lot.

"I wasn't chasing him. I wouldn't chase a man. I'm done with men, remember?"

She lifts her eyebrows. "Are you going to tell me why you're done with men?"

And reveal what an idiot I was for falling for a man who was a liar, a cheat, and a thief? Yeah, no, I pass.

She sighs. "The reason you're done with men is off the table. For now. Back to why you stopped chasing Jaxon."

"I wasn't chasing him."

She giggles. "Did you forget how I caught you standing outside the men's bathroom waiting for Jaxon to exit?"

"He was in there thirty minutes. I was worried about his health."

"What about the time you blocked his car in? He couldn't leave until you moved your car."

"It was an accident."

It wasn't an accident and Jaxon did leave before I moved my car. He got a ride home with Kai, who was mad at me for gifting him a calendar. Okay, it was five different calendars. And a watch. And a stopwatch.

"And then there was the time you disabled the Wi-fi from the entire distillery, thinking he would come out of his office to check what happened."

He didn't check what happened. He used his phone as a hotspot. Doesn't he know how much it costs to use your phone as a hotspot for the entire day?

"But the best was when you switched off all of the electricity for the entire distillery."

I didn't switch off *all of the* electricity. I would never endanger the beer or whiskey.

"Rhett and the rest of the Raider brothers had a bet going on how long Jaxon would stay in his office before he realized the electricity was out."

How was I to know Jaxon has a mini-generator for his office?

"Who won the bet?"

Dakota shakes her finger at me. "Don't try and get me off the subject. Why are you giving up on Jaxon?"

"Seriously? You have to ask after listing all the ways I tried to get his attention and all the ways he managed to ignore me. The poor man would rather have hemorrhoids than speak to me. Case closed."

"But you seemed really into him."

I was. I still relive our one kiss every night in bed. It gets me all hot and bothered every time.

"I thought he could be my rebound man," I say instead of admitting how embarrassed I am to admit the man who I wanted to strip naked and taste every inch of ignored me the following day.

Dakota pats my hand. "I thought Rhett would be my rebound."

I grab onto the change of subject. "But he's not. He's your forever man."

"Yeah." She sighs.

I pull into the parking lot of *Sirens & Saddles* and find a spot. I'm actually terrified of riding a horse. But I figure being terrified will get my mind off of Jaxon. I can't be scared of being bucked off a horse and breaking my neck while daydreaming about his lips, can I?

No one's that good of a multitasker.

Chapter 8

"Welp. That didn't turn out the way I expected."
~ Blossom

TWO MONTHS LATER

Blossom

I glance at the clock. Thirty minutes. I have less than half an hour to finish this inventory, order any missing supplies, and get changed for Dakota's party. I can do this.

Ha! I throw my arms in the air in celebration when I finish ordering the supplies in less than twenty minutes. Ten minutes to change. More than I need.

There's a knock on the restroom door when I'm applying my lipstick. "Blossom, are you ready?"

I open the door and beam at my boss. "With five minutes to spare."

Paisley shakes her head. "Your obsession with time management rivals mine."

"There's a reason you hired me."

We walk out of the brewery – the real brewery that has been rebuilt to its original glory – to my car. We moved the brewing facilities of *Five Fathoms Brewing* back to its original location a month ago.

And I'm not sad to miss seeing Jaxon every day. I don't miss those geeky t-shirts stretched over his chest. Or his hair sticking up in every direction. Or those ocean blue eyes. And especially not those nerdy glasses. I don't miss any of it!

"I hope everything works out between Rhett and Dakota," I say as I drive toward the *Hideaway Haven Resort*.

Rhett really messed up and broke Dakota's heart. But he's determined to win her back. Despite my past, I'm siding with love. I do hope he convinces her to forgive him.

"Rhett is a Raider. He'll convince Dakota to give him another chance."

I smirk at her. "You sound experienced."

"Eli is very persuasive." As evidenced by the fact that she's now living with him.

My stomach cramps but I ignore it. I'm happy for my friends. I am. Paisley and Dakota deserve all the happiness in the world. It's not their fault I'm obsessed with a Raider brother who pretends I don't exist.

We arrive at *Hideaway Haven Resort* and make our way to the restaurant. I gawk at my surroundings. The resort is super fancy and not somewhere I can usually afford to visit. Although, I could afford it if…

Nope, not thinking about him today. Today should be a happy occasion. And not a trip down hell lane.

I frown when I notice the Raider brothers are waiting in the hallway outside the restaurant. "What's going on?"

Eli points inside. "Rhett is still groveling."

Miles chuckles. "It's hilarious."

"We should have planted a microphone at their table," Zane says.

Kai sighs. "I tried. The hostess wouldn't take a bribe."

Only one Raider brother doesn't speak – Jaxon. He fiddles with his glasses. Why are his nerdy tendencies sexy? Since when am I into nerds? The jeans hugging his hips don't scream nerd, though. No, they scream for me to touch him. I clutch my purse instead.

"Uh oh," Miles mutters and I force my thoughts away from Jaxon. He doesn't deserve my attention anyway. "Dakota's crying."

"Those are happy tears," Paisley says.

"How can you tell?" Zane pushes his way to the front. "Oh."

"Oh, what?" I elbow my way through the brothers. "Ah," I say when I catch the couple making out.

Kai smirks. "Time to interrupt." He marches through the restaurant with Miles and Zane hot on his heels.

I chase after them. "Can't you let them kiss for a while?"

"And miss the fun of disturbing them?" Zane asks.

He has a point.

"Hey!" Kai shouts when we reach their table and they startle apart.

"What's going on?" Dakota asks.

I throw my arms in the air. "We're here to celebrate your relationship!"

Jaxon flinches, and I glare at him. "Excuse me. I'm sorry it's impossible for you to pretend I don't exist when I shout."

"I'm not pretending you don't exist."

I snort. "Liar. Liar. Pants on fire."

Jaxon lifts his glasses and pinches his nose. I refuse to think the gesture is adorable. Re-fuse! "I'm not a liar."

"Seriously? You pretended to be invisible to avoid me."

Paisley glances back and forth between us. "I'm confused. I thought you were hooking up in the distillery."

Why would she think we're hooking up? She saw us kiss once. And she hasn't mentioned it since. We work together every day. And we're friends. There's no way if our situation was reversed, I wouldn't have fired five hundred questions at her.

A blush covers Jaxon's face. "It was a mistake."

"A mistake?" I screech. "I'm a mistake?"

I'll put up with a lot of shit from a man. As evidenced by my asshole ex who I should have left long before he cheated on me. But saying I'm a mistake? No way. Nuh huh. I have more pride than to be referred to as a mistake.

I spin around and march out of the restaurant. I do not want to breathe the same air as Jaxon right now. He can fall off of a cliff for all I care. Would it be wrong if I pushed him? Probably. Stupid morals.

"Blossom!" Jaxon shouts.

I glance behind me to discover him chasing me. Now, he chases me? When we're in a crowded resort with all of his family as witnesses?

Two can play at his hide-and-seek game. I scan the hallway I'm running down. There. An open door.

I rush inside and slam the door shut behind me. Jaxon will never find me now.

"Blossom?"

Mother fluffing ducks not in a row. Speaking of exes. I close my eyes and hope I'm hallucinating due to lack of oxygen from running. I really should work out more.

"Is that you, Blossom?"

Damn. No such luck. I force a smile on my face and spin around.

"Alan. What are you doing here?"

He chuckles. "I was about to ask you the same thing."

"I live on Smuggler's Hideaway." My cheeks are beginning to ache from how hard I'm forcing this fake smile.

"I wondered where you were living."

I bet. It's difficult to harass someone when you don't know where they live. Although, his lawyer manages to harass me enough.

"Welp. Here I am." I throw my arms in the air. "What are you doing here?"

I cross my fingers behind my back. *Please don't say you're moving here. Please don't say you're moving here.* Talk about a disaster in the making. Or should I say homicide? My morals don't give a flying seal about throwing Alan off a cliff.

Alan grins. "I'm getting married here."

"Here? As in on the island of Smuggler's Hideaway?"

"In this very resort."

Bleeping smugglers drowning in the sea. Thanks for the reminder that things can always get worse.

"Congratulations! Where's your future wife?" I scan the room, which I now realize is filled with all things bridal – sample bouquets, various champagnes, a plethora of cakes, etc.

"Stacey hasn't arrived yet."

At least he's not marrying the tramp he cheated on me with. Why do I care? I don't. I don't care who the cheating asshole is marrying. I care about getting the devil out of here.

"Too bad. I would have loved to meet her." I nearly pat myself on the back with how true my lie sounds.

"You can meet her. Why don't you come to the wedding?"

Has he lost his hold on sanity? Why the hell would I want to come to his wedding?

"And I can meet your husband," he continues.

Well, shit. Now I know why he wants me to come to his wedding.

When I hesitate, his eyes narrow. Why I ever thought his brown eyes were handsome is anyone's guess. How did I not notice the calculating gleam there?

"There is a husband, isn't there?"

I don't hesitate to lie. Trust me. This lie is more than necessary. "Of course, there is."

There's a knock on the door. "Blossom, are you in there?"

"There he is now."

I open the door and haul Jaxon to me. "Look who I ran into, honey bunches of oats."

"Um…"

I widen my eyes in a plea for his help. His ocean blue eyes fill with confusion. Nothing new there.

"How would I know who you ran into? You were hiding from me."

I force out a giggle. "Because I enjoy it when you chase me."

Alan steps forward and offers Jaxon his hand. "I'm Alan."

"Jaxon." They shake. Jaxon looks adorably confused while Alan appears annoyed.

"You don't know who I am?" Alan demands. I nearly roll my eyes. Who does he think he is? A superstar? Being the best salesperson at a tire store does not make you a superstar.

"Should I?"

"I'm Alan," my ex announces.

"Yes, you said."

I sputter out a laugh, and Alan glares at me. "Sorry. Jaxon isn't very good with names," I manage to explain between my bouts of laughter.

Alan narrows his eyes on Jaxon as he studies him. "But I'm your ex. Your husband should know your ex-boyfriend's name."

Jaxon's eyes widen. Before he can open his mouth and prove I'm a liar, Terri, the event coordinator for the resort, sweeps into the room.

"I'm sorry," she says as she lays some lacy material over the table. "I think this is the color you want."

I grasp Jaxon's hand and back out of the room. "We'll get out of your hair."

"I'll see you next weekend," Alan yells after me as I flee the room.

"Next weekend?" Jaxon asks when the door is closed behind us.

I glance around to ensure no one's eavesdropping before answering. "At his wedding."

He skids to a stop. "His wedding?"

I gulp. "He kind of invited us."

"Us? Why would he invite us?" Understanding lights his blue eyes. "Because he believes we're married. Why did you tell him we're married?"

"It's a long story."

He consults his watch. "I have time now. Please explain."

"Well…"

Chapter 9

"This must be what people mean when they say opportunity knocks." ~ Jaxon

Jaxon

Blossom bites her lip as she studies me. I want to remove her teeth and replace them with mine. I shove my hands in my pockets before I reach for her.

"Why did you tell your ex we're married?" I push when she doesn't speak.

"It doesn't matter."

"It doesn't matter? He thinks we're coming to his wedding next weekend."

She waves her hand in dismissal. "He'll forget he invited us. Alan doesn't follow through unless it benefits him somehow."

A woman hurries down the hallway. She was in the room with us and Alan, but I don't know who she is. She stops in front of Blossom. "Here." She hands her an envelope.

"What's this?" Blossom asks.

"Mr. Simmons wanted me to make sure you have an invitation to the wedding next week. No need to RSVP. I'll add you to the list."

Blossom's smile is forced. "Thanks, Terri."

Terri waves as she rushes back to the room with Blossom's ex.

"Mermaids drowning in the sea," Blossom mutters. "I really thought he'd forget."

"Why does he think you're married?"

"It's okay. You don't have to come to the wedding with me. In fact, I won't go." She nods as if the matter is settled. The matter is not settled.

"Why did you tell your ex we're married?"

"It doesn't matter." She pivots on her heel but I capture her wrist before she can escape.

"Blossom." Her body shivers and I realize I'm caressing her wrist with my thumb. I drop her hand and step away. I immediately miss the feel of her silky skin.

"Tell me what's going on," I demand.

"You can't demand to know what's going on after ignoring me for months," she hisses at me. "I'm a mistake, remember?"

"I didn't say you're a mistake. I said kissing you was a mistake."

Pain flashes in her brown eyes.

"Forget I said anything. I'm an asshole."

She snorts. "You won't hear me arguing with you."

"Come on." I herd her down the hallway. "Let's go somewhere private and discuss this."

"You want to discuss why you ignored me for two months?"

No. I want to discuss why she lied to her ex. I need to know why she's afraid of attending his wedding. Does she still have feelings for him? My stomach curls as jealousy fills me. Blossom isn't mine to be jealous of but my body doesn't care.

We pass an alcove with two chairs. I coax Blossom into a chair and sit across from her.

"Why did you tell your ex you're married to me?"

"Wow. No small talk. No asking how I'm doing. Just bam! Straight to the point."

I frown. "I don't understand small talk."

"Of course, you don't." She motions to my t-shirt and I glance down to read it. This one says *Hi, I'm good. Thanks. There. Now we don't need to make small talk.*

"Blossom, you pulled me into this situation by saying we're married. And now we're invited to your ex's wedding next weekend. If you want my help, you need to tell me what's going on."

She scowls. "Who said I want your help? I told you I won't be attending the wedding."

"And what kind of message will your absence send?"

Her nose wrinkles. "Message?"

"You told this man you're married. I assume there's a good reason you lied."

"There is. I promise."

"If you don't show up at his wedding, he might figure out you're lying. What happens then?"

She gasps and clutches her chest. "He can't figure out I'm lying. He can't."

I capture her hand and squeeze. "Why? What will he do?" I feel her pulse race. She's obviously terrified of this man. I growl. "What did he do to you?"

"It's not what you think."

"He didn't hurt you?"

She ducks her head. "Not physically."

I pinch her chin and force her to meet my gaze. "There are more ways to hurt a person than physically."

"I know," she whispers.

I want to find Alan and bash his face in. How dare he cause this vibrant woman to be afraid? But I can't abandon Blossom. Not when she's hurting. I want to pull her into my arms and kiss her until she forgets all about any other man who came before me. Let alone, Alan the asshole.

I've been fighting Blossom's pull from the first time she told me she doesn't have cooties. I can't have her, but I can help her.

"Let's go to the wedding."

She blinks at me. "What?"

"Let's go to the wedding."

"Why?"

"Let's show Alan the asshole he did not break you. In fact, you leveled up."

She giggles the way I intended her to. "Leveled up? With you?"

I puff out my chest. "With me. Trust me. I clean up nice."

Her gaze dips to my chest and she bites her bottom lip. My cock twitches. It wants to play with those pretty lips. Feel them surrounding it. It hardens and lengthens as visions of her on her knees in front of me flash through my mind.

"Do you have an outfit that doesn't include a nerdy t-shirt?"

I draw a hand down my chest. "You don't like my t-shirts?"

I'm playing with fire. This woman can't be mine. She's too tempting. She causes me to act out of character. My body's reaction to her isn't normal. I should leave well enough alone.

But I won't. I will give her a weekend to remember. And afterwards we'll go our separate ways. Again.

She wags the invitation at me. "The wedding is black tie."

"It's a good thing I own a tuxedo."

Her eyes widen. I could drown in those light brown eyes. The deep gold reminds me of a smoky whiskey. I do love a good smoky whiskey.

"You own a tuxedo?"

"My brother's a billionaire."

"And you're a millionaire."

I'm not sure if she's asking, but I nod. The distillery is doing extremely well. I refuse to be ashamed about having money. Not after how we struggled after Dad abandoned us.

"Okay," she gives in. "We'll go to the wedding."

I reach for my phone. "I'll reserve a chalet for the weekend."

She places a hand on my wrist to stop me. "We don't need a chalet for the weekend. We live on the island. We can go home after the wedding."

I smirk. "But if we stay in a chalet for the weekend, it'll give us a better chance to rub our relationship in Alan's face."

"I never knew you were this devious."

"Have you met my brothers? I wouldn't survive in the Raider family without being a little devious."

She grins. "I like this side of you."

"The matter is settled. We'll stay in a chalet next weekend for the wedding."

"Can't we book a room?" Her nose wrinkles. "The chalets are super expensive."

I kiss her adorable nose. "I'm paying."

"You are not paying."

"I'm your husband. I'm paying."

"Jaxon," she growls. It's cute. I have to bite my tongue before I laugh at how cute she is. Somehow, I don't think she'd appreciate me laughing at her.

"Blossom."

"Seriously, Jaxon. I don't care how much money you have. You're not spending it on a chalet at this fancy schmancy resort because of me."

"Why not because of you?"

"Duh." She rolls her eyes. "You don't like me."

"I like you just fine." More than just fine, actually but I can't give Blossom any hope. Our relationship will never be more than friendship, despite how my body yearns for hers.

"Geez, hubby. Careful how romantic you get. I might not be able to handle it. I might end up jumping you right here and now."

She's joking but my cock doesn't realize it. It urges me to take Blossom up on her offer. *Jump her! Jump her!*

I ignore my cock. It's usually not difficult to ignore my physical urges. But with Blossom, I have to grit my teeth and force myself to calm the hell down before I do something I regret.

"We'll save the jumping each other for this weekend when we have privacy."

Her mouth drops open. "Jaxon Raider, did you just make a joke?"

"I can make jokes." Not often and not very well but I'm not completely inept. Socially awkward? There's no denying it. But even the most socially awkward person can laugh and joke sometimes.

"Maybe this weekend won't be terrible after all."

I squeeze her hand. "This weekend will be wonderful. I promise."

"You don't have to do this. Alan is my problem."

Anyone who causes my vibrant Blossom to dim is my problem to deal with. I can't have her for myself, but no one is hurting her on my watch. No one.

"I agreed to help you. The matter is closed."

She stands. "I thank you, good sir. For your services." She curtseys. "But I will pay you back," she mutters before walking off.

As I watch her retreat, I realize she deftly avoided answering my questions.

I still don't know what Alan did. But I will find out.

Chapter 10

"It's no fun being on the other side of the gossipmongering." ~ Blossom

BLOSSOM

Knock! Knock! Knock!

"We know you're in there!" Dakota shouts through the door.

I hurry to open the front door before she wakes up the entire apartment building. Considering most of the apartments are vacation rentals used by visitors who think it's 'fun' to test how strong the Smuggler's Hideaway moonshine is, waking up my neighbors is not a good idea. There's a limit to how many times I'm willing to clean vomit from the hallway carpet.

"I never denied being home."

Paisley's nose wrinkles. "We expected you to."

I know exactly why they expected me to, but I'm not afraid of my friends asking questions. Doesn't mean I'll answer them. But I'm not a scaredy cat who hides.

I usher them inside my apartment. "What's up? We didn't make plans for today."

Diverting their attention isn't hiding, FYI.

Dakota giggles. "You seriously think you can disappear from my party with Jaxon – the man of your dreams – for several hours and not think we'll show up at your door the next day?"

I hold up a finger. "One, Jaxon is not the man of my dreams."

"Liar," Paisley mutters but I ignore her.

I hold up a second finger. "And, two, I did not disappear for hours."

Dakota rolls her eyes. "You were gone forever."

Paisley sighs. "Uh oh."

"Do not exaggerate time by using the word forever incorrectly. We've discussed how important timekeeping and time management are."

Dakota holds up her hand. "I am not having another conversation with you about the importance of time management. I'm still having flashbacks from the previous one."

Paisley clears her throat. "We're here to find out what's going on with you and Jaxon."

I lift my eyebrow. "I thought you knew. We have an 'arrangement'."

Her cheeks darken and she dips her chin. "Sorry. I've been preoccupied. I shouldn't have assumed."

I let it go. Between the hurricane, relocating the brewing facilities, and her tango with Eli, she has been extremely busy.

Dakota elbows me. "What is going on between the two of you?"

I'm not getting out of this conversation. Not considering the way I badgered Dakota when she was being wooed by Rhett. Payback's a bitch. But I can use this to my advantage.

"I'll tell you if you agree to go on an adventure with me."

Dakota moans. "The last adventure I agreed to go on with you ended up with you fighting a horse."

"I did not fight a horse."

"You yelled at the poor thing and called it names."

"Poor thing? It was stubborn and refused to move when I gently asked it to."

"It moved just fine when Warren whistled at it."

"Warren – aka Mr. I'll Own *Sirens & Saddles* once my dad is gone – was creepy."

"He's always been creepy," Paisley says.

I shiver. "Creepy how?"

"We caught him trying to drill a hole into the wall of the girls' locker room. I hope he's better with horses than he is with drills because he had no clue what he was doing."

"Good thing you caught him," I say. I am never going to *Sirens & Saddles* again. To avoid Warren, not because me and horseback riding do not go together.

Dakota scowls. "Those poor horses. They have to be around a creep."

"Should we rescue them?" I ask. I'm up for a rescue mission. Anything to get my mind off my real problems.

"And put them where?" Dakota scans my apartment. "You don't exactly have room here."

Technically, I have the money to build a ranch for the horses. But I don't want to touch *that* money any more than I have to. Touching it would confirm they're gone. Plus, my lawyer says I shouldn't use the money until the Alan situation is solved.

"Can we stop discussing rescuing horses and get back to the matter at hand?" Paisley asks.

I rub my hands together. "What adventure are we going on?"

Paisley sighs. "You're as bad as Sophia, Chloe, Nova, and Maya."

Those are the women she founded *Five Fathoms Brewing* with. The five are the best of friends and get up to all kinds of trouble. They're my heroes.

"And you're innocent?" Dakota asks. "You didn't get the Raider brothers drunk at *Mermaid Mystical Gardens* and get kicked out of the amusement park?"

Paisley's lips purse. "We did not get kicked out."

"Sure, you didn't." Dakota pats her shoulder while mouthing to me, *she totally got kicked out.*

"If you two don't pick an adventure, I will."

"It's a beautiful day for the boardwalk," Dakota offers.

"The boardwalk? How is the boardwalk an adventure?"

She giggles. "You'll figure out a way to make an adventure of it. I have faith in you."

I bow to her. "I appreciate your faith in me."

I herd them toward the door, and soon enough, we're nearing the boardwalk. It's less than a five-minute walk from my apartment since I live smackdab in the middle of Smuggler's Rest, which is pretty much on the ocean.

"What game should we play first?" I ask.

"I didn't agree to games," Dakota says.

"What else is there to do?" I motion toward all the gaming halls.

"We could have coffee and you could tell us what's going on with you and Jaxon."

Paisley snorts. "She's not talking unless we play a game. We can't play balloon dart. Dakota will end up killing someone."

Dakota glares at her. "I've never killed anyone with a dart."

"But you have caused bloody noses."

"Now, I want to play balloon dart. Can I pick whose nose you bloody up?" I ask.

Paisley snorts. "I doubt it since she can't aim."

"It was an accident," Dakota insists.

Paisley pats her shoulder. "It's okay to be accident-prone. Not everyone can have my prowess with darts."

"Oh, those are fighting words. I bet I can beat you at basketball shootout." I grin. This is going to be fun.

Paisley rolls her shoulders back. "I accept your bet."

Dakota pushes her way in between us. "Hold on. You two can play kiddie games as much as you want. *After* Blossom tells us what's happening with Jaxon. Because the last thing Blossom told me was that she was giving up on him."

"I did give up on him. There's nothing happening between us."

Paisley crosses her arms over her chest. "You're not attending a wedding together this weekend?"

I gasp. "How do you know?"

Dakota's gaze ping pongs between me and Paisley. "It's true? You're attending a wedding with Jaxon?"

I consider lying. It's not as if they're going to be at the wedding.

"Before you make up some bullshit, I already spoke to Terri and she confirmed you were invited to the wedding. She handed the invitation to you herself. While you were standing next to Jaxon."

I glare at Paisley. "Did you seriously hunt down the resort event planner for gossip?"

"I may have accidentally overheard when Terri phoned Eli and asked what his geeky brother's name was for the place cards for the wedding this weekend."

"Jaxon's a nerd, not a geek," I mutter.

She ignores me. "Nonetheless, you are attending a wedding at *Hideaway Haven Resort* this weekend with Jaxon?"

I blow out a breath. "Yes, I am."

"But you were done chasing Jaxon," Dakota says.

I waggle my eyebrows at her. "Maybe he chased me."

"It's true." Paisley nods. "Jaxon did chase you out of the restaurant."

Dakota narrows her eyes on me. "There's more to this story."

"Fine." I huff. "The groom is my ex, who cheated on me and Jaxon agreed to help me show him I leveled up."

All true. Not the entire truth, but true.

Dakota throws her hands in the air. "Why didn't you say so in the first place?"

I roll my eyes. "The same way you told us about your dead husband."

Her shoulders hunch. "Oh, yeah."

"Now." I shove her toward the basketball shootout game. "It's time for me to win my bet with Paisley."

"You can try," Paisley sings.

We pay and line up at three hoops games next to each other.

"Ready, set, go," I shout and grab my first basketball. I don't pay attention to Dakota or Paisley as I sink ball after ball into the hoop. Dakota isn't a threat anyway. And what Paisley doesn't know is, I played on the basketball team in high school. I got this.

"Ow! My nose!" Someone shouts and I glance over my shoulder.

A man is standing with a hand covering his nose while blood pours down his face. Dakota rushes to him with Paisley and me hot on her heels.

"I'm sorry. I don't know what happened. The basketball slipped out of my hands." Dakota reaches for him but he steps back.

"There's a first aid station a block away next to *The Salty Siren*." Paisley points toward the red cross sign.

He hurries off. "I'm sorry!" Dakota shouts after him.

"I have to admire your aim," Paisley tells her.

Dakota's eyes widen. "What?"

"Whether you use a dart or a basketball, you go straight for the nose." Paisley laughs and I join her.

Dakota and Paisley came to my apartment to snoop into my love life. What they don't realize is, they offered me a reprieve from all the questions swirling around in my mind.

Does Jaxon want me? Or is he just being nice?

Does Alan believe I'm married? Will he drop the lawsuit now?

Spending the weekend with the man I want, who obviously doesn't want me, is going to be difficult. But if the result is Alan dropping the lawsuit, it'll be worth all the sexual frustration.

Chapter 11

"Maybe having brothers isn't such a bad thing after all." ~ Jaxon

JAXON

I drag my feet as I make my way from my car to Eli's mansion. Today is the monthly Raider poker night, and I'm required to attend.

I've tried everything I can think of to get out of attending. I've feigned being sick. Miles hauled me out of bed, Zane handed me a bucket to 'barf' in, and Kai dragged me to the poker table. I've claimed to be too busy with work. But Eli shut off all the power to the distillery – including my back-up generator I didn't think he knew about.

I was certain when I 'lost' my good luck charm, I'd finally figured out a way to skip poker night. Since we're required to bring a good luck charm to each poker night. I didn't expect Rhett to comb through my house until he found the Green King – my Chia Pet that resembles Elvis.

The door flies open, and Miles, Kai, and Zane pour outside.

"I win! Pay up, suckers!" Miles shouts.

Kai glares at me. "You let me down."

"You're always trying to get out of poker night, but now you come?" Zane complains before slapping a ten-dollar bill in Miles's hand.

I ignore them and enter the house. They follow me and we gather in Eli's living room with Rhett and Eli, who are standing near the bar.

"Didn't think you could make it," Rhett says.

I hug my Chia Pet close to my chest. "I didn't want to give you an excuse to kidnap the Green King again."

"It doesn't resemble Elvis in the least," Miles grumbles.

I glare at him. "I won the science fair."

Zane snorts. "Because you had a fifty-page PowerPoint presentation on how to grow plants. The judges gave you the prize to shut you up."

"It was fifty-five pages," I correct.

"Dude." Miles chuckles. "You're not making this any better."

"Says the man holding what he claims is a rabbit's foot but is not the size of a rabbit."

Miles pets the furry foot. "Don't make fun of Hopper. He's sensitive."

"He's a freak, is what he is," Rhett mumbles.

Kai points at him. "You're holding a bowling shoe. You're not one to talk."

Eli rolls his eyes. "As if you're one to talk with your pickle in a jar."

"Do not make fun of Mr. Crisp. He can out poker all of you."

Zane sighs. "Me and Nugget don't need this negativity."

"Nugget?" Miles snorts. "It's a taxidermized squirrel in a cowboy hat."

"Can't we get rid of this requirement to bring a good luck charm?" I ask.

Zane narrows his eyes on me. "We'll get rid of the good luck charms when you stop insisting on the 'Jaxon' rule of poker."

I clear my throat and push my glasses up my nose. "The bluff shot rule is everyone's favorite."

The bluff shot rule works as follows. If someone catches you bluffing and calls it out, they get to invent a one-time rule for the next hand. The one-time rule can be anything. Each of my brothers has a favorite outrageous rule.

Miles invented the Mermaid's Mercy Rule. If a player draws three hearts in a row, he has to sing a sea shanty before the next round begins. If he doesn't, he folds.

Eli came up with the Smuggler's Bluff. Each player has to call out a card in their hand. If they get caught lying, they have to reveal a secret.

Kai's favorite is the Talk Like a Pirate. Everyone has to talk like a pirate and if they don't, they forfeit the round.

Zane's rule is the Siren's Curse. If anyone draws the Queen of Hearts, they're cursed and have to end every sentence with "arrr" until someone else draws a queen.

Only Rhett doesn't have an outrageous rule. My brothers think I'm the boring one, but Rhett can be a stick in the mud when it comes to cards and money. He's very serious about money. It's probably why he's the CFO of the distillery.

"Can we please stop talking about poker?" Zane asks.

I frown. "It's poker night. What else would we discuss besides poker?"

He rolls his eyes. "How about why you're attending a wedding as Blossom's plus one this weekend."

My brow wrinkles. "How do you know?"

Eli clears his throat. "The event coordinator at *Hideaway Haven Resort* phoned me to ask what your name is."

"Why does she need to know my name?"

He raises an eyebrow. "Because you're attending Alan and Stacey's wedding this weekend and she needs your name for the place cards."

"Place cards?"

"Are you serious?" Zane asks. "Even I know place cards are placed at your assigned seat at a wedding."

"He's stalling," Kai says.

"What am I stalling about?"

Miles taps his chin. "I don't think he's stalling. I think he's genuinely confused."

"What am I supposed to be confused about? What am I missing?" I hate when I don't understand what's happening. But I should be used to it. My brothers love to speak in riddles.

Eli shoves a glass of whiskey in my hand. "We want to know what's going on with you and Blossom."

"Nothing's going on."

Rhett crosses his arms over his chest. "You're accompanying her to a wedding and nothing's going on?"

My nose wrinkles. "Why do you appear mad?"

"Because Blossom is Dakota's best friend."

"I'm aware."

Zane throws an arm around my shoulders. "Rhett loves Dakota. Dakota loves Blossom. Therefore, if you hurt Blossom, you hurt Dakota and Rhett gets mad."

"I understand the logic." I clear my throat. "But I am not hurting Blossom. I'm helping her."

Miles chuckles. "This ought to be good."

I frown at him. "There's nothing funny about this."

Zane squeezes my shoulder. "He doesn't mean the current situation. He means the fallout."

"The fallout?"

"You'll see," he mutters before dropping his arm and strolling to the bar and pouring himself a glass of whiskey.

"How are you helping Blossom?" Rhett asks.

"I believe Blossom wishes to keep the situation private."

He steps closer. "You're not helping her show her ex that she leveled up with you?"

"Why are you asking all of these questions if you already know the answers?"

"Hold on. What did Blossom's ex do to her?" Eli asks.

I shrug since I don't know what Alan did. I know it's bad. He hurt her in some way. I just don't know how. I intend to find out this weekend, though. And afterwards, I'll get revenge for her.

"I don't like this."

"Because Paisley and Blossom are friends?" I guess.

"Because Blossom is one of us. A smuggler," he says and my brothers nod in agreement.

Huh. I didn't expect my brothers to want to help Blossom. I know they like her. It's impossible not to like her. She's smart and fun. She practically radiates happiness when she smiles. She's everything I'm not.

But she's also a newcomer to the island. Usually, the only people referred to as smugglers are those who grew up on the island. For good reason, mainlanders can't be trusted to stay.

Just ask my dad. Except you can't, since he left when I was fourteen and hasn't been heard from since.

"Should we stay at the resort this weekend?" Miles asks. "We can act as moral support."

"Good idea," Zane says. "We can give Jaxon moral support since someone hates crowds, and a wedding is a crowd."

I frown. I don't hate crowds. I don't enjoy them either. But I can handle a crowd. Assuming I don't have to make small talk to dozens of people.

Rhett groans. "You just want to crash the wedding."

Miles shrugs. "What can I say? Desperate bridesmaids is a thing."

"I can't make it this weekend," Kai says and everyone switches his attention to him.

"Why not?" Zane asks before slapping his thigh. "I nearly forgot. You have a date with Harper. Oh, wait. No, you don't, since she won't give you the time of day."

"Harper? The owner of the *Rumrunner?*" I ask. "Isn't she ten years older than you?"

Miles clutches his chest. "Age is merely a number when love is involved."

Kai shoves him. "It's not love. And she's seven years older than me. Not ten."

"Dude, if you're merely horny, come to the wedding with me. We'll score a couple of chicks. I promise you'll have a good time." Miles waggles his eyebrows.

"The wedding? You're not coming to the wedding."

I don't understand what's happening between Blossom and her ex, but I'm certain she doesn't want everyone to know. Especially not my brothers, who think gossiping is a sport they're determined to win.

Eli sidles up to me. "Don't worry. I'll keep them away from the wedding."

"Unless you need us," Rhett adds. "If you do, all you need to do is call."

"We've got your back, brother," Eli says.

"Always," Rhett agrees.

I lift my chin in thanks. I shouldn't be surprised. Rhett and Eli have always been there for me.

After Dad abandoned us for the mainland, Eli worked side jobs to ensure we had money for the 'extra' stuff. A chemistry set for me. Sports stuff for my younger brothers.

And Rhett took over as parent of the family since Mom was working two jobs to make ends meet. He made sure I had quiet to study. Not an easy task when your younger brothers are Miles, Zane, and Kai.

Their words are a good reminder. I don't have a dad. But I have my brothers – who have always been there for me.

Chapter 12

"Welp. That wasn't awkward at all." ~ Blossom

BLOSSOM

As I carry my suitcase toward my car, Jaxon drives up in his vintage Mustang and parks next to me. I open my trunk and place my suitcase in it.

He steps out of his car. "What are you doing?"

I frown at him. "Isn't it obvious? I'm putting my suitcase in my trunk."

"You're not driving."

I rear back. "Excuse me?"

"We're driving together."

"I can drive myself."

"Won't it seem odd to Alan if we show up separately since we're supposed to be married?"

Flying seals. He's right. I bend to pick up my suitcase but he nudges me out of the way. "I've got it."

"Are you going to be a gentleman all weekend?"

"Of course. You're my wife. A man should be a gentleman to his wife."

I wish other men thought the way he does.

"I'm only pretending to be your wife," I say, since I need the reminder that this isn't real. This is fake. Jaxon doesn't care about me. He's helping me out because he's a good guy. As evidenced by him putting my suitcase in his trunk.

"Why is your suitcase this heavy?"

Probably because I put every nice outfit I own in it. I need to make sure I have an outfit for every occasion. I will not get caught out in ratty jeans. Not this girl.

"It's a mystery," I claim as I reach for the car handle.

Jaxon bats my hand out of the way. "I open the door for you."

I hold up my hands. "Don't expect to hear me complain. You want to spoil me? Spoil away."

"I enjoy spoiling you," he says before shutting the door.

Weird. He didn't sound as if he was playing a role. He's good at this acting thing. I didn't expect the nerdy whiskey distiller to be a good actor.

"Were you in drama club in high school?" I ask as we drive away from my apartment building.

"Drama club? I did not have time for drama club."

He must be a natural born actor. Good to know.

I peruse the invitation as we drive. "An entire wedding weekend is over the top, don't you think?"

"You don't want a wedding weekend?"

I scrunch up my nose in distaste. "A welcome lunch for the guests, an afternoon wine tasting, a Friday night dinner followed by karaoke, spa day Saturday, the actual wedding,

wedding party with dinner and dancing, and a Sunday champagne brunch. It's a bit much, isn't it?"

"What would your ideal wedding be?"

I stare out the window as I contemplate the answer. "I've always imagined getting married barefoot on the beach. The only people in attendance would be my closest friends."

"No family?"

My heart spasms. I would dearly love my parents to be in attendance. But they're gone.

I wish they'd lived long enough for me to wise up and ditch Alan. Mom always disliked him, and Dad didn't trust him. I thought they were overreacting. They weren't.

"No family," I whisper.

He catches my hand and squeezes. "Sorry. I didn't mean to bring up bad memories."

I cling to his hand. "It's okay. You didn't know."

No one on Smuggler's Hideaway knows. I haven't told my friends about my parents. If I did, I'd have to explain all the rest about Alan as well and I'm not ready to admit how stupid I was.

"We're here," Jaxon says as we pull into the resort. He parks but he doesn't get out. He swivels to meet my gaze. "Are you sure you want to be here?"

I roll my eyes. "Kind of late now, isn't it?"

"No. It's not. If you want to leave, we leave. It's really quite simple."

To him, it probably is simple. But not to me. If I prove to Alan I'm married, he'll realize he doesn't have a chance to win the lawsuit and drop it. I'm more than ready for the dark cloud of this lawsuit to move away and let sun shine on my life again.

"I want to be here."

"Okay." He nods.

I sit still as he rounds the front of the vehicle and comes to open my door. He offers me his hand and I accept.

A zap of electricity hits me when we touch. Judging by Jaxon's widened eyes, he feels it, too. Sexual tension fills the air as we stare at each other.

"Do you need help with your bags?" A porter asks and – pop! – there goes the tension.

While Jaxon helps the porter with the bags, I make my way inside to the reception desk.

"I'm Wesley," the man behind the desk introduces himself. "How can I assist you this morning?"

"Checking in. The reservation should be under the name Raider."

Checking in under Jaxon's name makes me feel all warm and fuzzy. How would it feel to add his name to mine permanently? And not as some ruse to fool my ex?

"We have you in one of our garden chalets," Wesley says.

"Chalet?" Alan whistles and I nearly jump. I didn't hear him approach. "It's a good thing we negotiated a discount for our wedding guests."

Jaxon slings an arm around my shoulders and draws me near. "A discount? We didn't get a discount."

"Oh, I'm sorry," Wesley says. "It doesn't say you're part of the wedding party in your reservation. I can add the discount now."

"It's fine," Jaxon says. "I forgot to say we're attending the wedding when I made the reservation."

Wesley hands him two key cards. "Here are your keys, Mr. and Mrs. Raider."

"Raider?" Alan raises his brow. "You said you'd never take a man's last name."

Jaxon kisses my forehead. "Funny. She never mentioned changing her name as a problem to me."

He's good. Who knew Jaxon, the nerd, would excel at being a fake husband? I wonder if he'd excel at being a real one.

Whoa. Where did that thought come from?

Concentrate on the present, Blossom. You've got enough issues without adding pining for your fake husband to the list.

Alan nods to my left hand. "But she wouldn't wear your ring either."

Jaxon sighs. "My petal doesn't like to wear rings." He frowns at my bare finger. "But I won't stop trying until she's wearing my ring."

I nearly shiver at the conviction in his voice. I might need to wear a chastity belt this weekend because there is no way I'm not jumping Jaxon if he continues this possessive gentleman routine.

"Maybe you haven't figured out the best way to persuade me yet," I tease.

Jaxon's eyes flare and butterflies erupt in my stomach. I am playing with fire here and I don't care. Let the flames burn me down. It'll be worth it to taste Jaxon again.

"A dare," he grumbles. "You know how much I enjoy a dare."

Alan clears his throat but I ignore him. I'm too busy being ensnared by ocean blue eyes to care about my ex. He tries again – this time much louder – and the moment is ruined.

"I'll see you two later. I need to speak to the owner, Hudson Clark." Alan smirks as he drops the name. Am I supposed to be impressed?

He starts toward Hudson but the former NFL player is already heading in our direction. Alan holds out his hand in greeting but Hudson passes him by and stops in front of us.

"Jaxon. I heard you were staying here this weekend."

They clap hands.

"Have you met my wife?" Jaxon asks.

Hudson's eyes light with amusement. Does he know the truth?

"Blossom, right? You work at the brewery."

Alan snorts from where he's lurking behind Hudson. "The brewery."

"The brewery where my wife also works," Hudson says in a loud voice.

Alan cringes at the rebuttal but it doesn't stop him for long. "Excuse me, Hudson. I have some questions about this week-end's activities."

"Terri will be happy to help you," Hudson says without bothering to look at him.

I bite my tongue before I burst into laughter at Alan's sour face. His nostrils flare as he glares at Hudson's back. He waits a few beats before finally stomping off.

"Is he gone?" Hudson whispers.

I erupt in laughter. "His face when you ignored him. I will love you forever for how you treated him."

Jaxon growls and I pet his chest to calm him without thinking.

Hudson's gaze flicks to my hand and I drop it. Oops. No touching the fake husband when not strictly necessary. Although, I'm the one who decides what's 'strictly necessary'.

"This is going to be fun," Hudson says before stalking off.

Jaxon drops his arm from around me. I immediately miss his touch. But then he catches my hand.

"Let's go find our chalet and get settled, Petal."

"Petal? Where does the nickname Petal come from?"

He shrugs. "Blossom. Petal. Seems obvious."

"A flower theme? I can live with it."

"What's your favorite flower?" he asks as we make our way out of the building and start walking the path toward the chalets.

"Tulips. I thought you hated small talk."

"Getting to know you isn't small talk," he says and I nearly melt.

Maybe pretending to be married to Jaxon for a weekend wasn't such a good idea after all. Because I don't know how long I can resist this gentleman act before I jump him.

I blow out a breath. No jumping your fake husband, Blossom. No matter how possessive and sweet he acts. It's not real. He's pretending.

Chapter 13

JAXON

We enter the chalet and I freeze. I fucked up. I assumed a 'chalet' would have multiple sleeping accommodations. I was wrong. There's one big bed and a small sofa I could never fit my six-foot-one frame onto.

After flirting with Blossom the entire morning, I'm ready to throw her onto the bed and find out how sturdy it is. I force my desire away. Blossom is not the woman for me. I can't chance falling for her only for her to leave when she's bored of me or the island.

"Wow." Blossom spins around and her blonde hair flies out behind her. "This place is awesome. I hope the discount from the wedding is fifty percent because this chalet cannot be cheap."

I don't give a shit what the discount is. Whatever the price of the chalet is, it's worth it to see Blossom happy. Her eyes twinkle, and her smile lights up her face. I'm drawn to her, but I manage to keep my feet planted where they are.

She pauses her twirling. "Holy mermaids," she breathes out before rushing to the sliding doors. She slams her palms against the glass. "There is an honest to smuggler hot tub out there. Good thing I brought my swimsuit."

She runs to her suitcase and flips it open.

"What are you doing?"

"Duh. I'm getting my swimsuit." She pauses to glance over her shoulder at me. "Unless you want to get into the hot tub without any clothes on."

My cock twitches with such vehemence I nearly fall over. Blossom in the hot tub without any clothes on? All those miles and miles of skin on display? Her perky breasts unconfined and ready to be touched? With my hands and mouth?

I inhale a deep breath and wrangle my hormones under control before I say to hell with it and throw Blossom over my shoulder.

"Don't we have the welcome lunch in less than an hour?" Her shoulders slump and I nearly kick myself for dimming her light. "We can skip the lunch."

"Nope." She squares her shoulders. "You didn't agree to spend the weekend with me romping around in the hot tub. You're here to play my husband."

I nearly growl at the word 'play' before I catch myself. Blossom isn't my wife. I'm not her husband. It is an act. We are playing. End of story.

She yanks a dress out of her suitcase. "I need thirty minutes to shower and change."

"Do you want me to change?"

I'm wearing khakis and a button-down shirt instead of my usual uniform of jeans and t-shirt. Eli and Rhett showed up at my house early this morning and picked out my 'wedding wardrobe'. The assholes think I don't know how to dress myself.

"You look good. I'll hurry."

She rushes to the bathroom and slams the door shut. Which is when I realize my second fuck up for the day. The wall between the shower and the bedroom is glass. Whoever is in the shower is clearly visible from the rest of the chalet.

My cock urges me to sit on the bed and enjoy the show. No matter how much I'm tempted, I would never violate Blossom's privacy in this way.

I grab a key card and escape the room.

I dig my ear pods out of my pocket and switch on a podcast to listen to as I wander around the resort. There's plenty of space to wander as the chalets are spaced a good distance apart to provide privacy to the guests. Considering Hudson caters to celebrities, it's necessary.

It's peaceful as I meander the paths through the gardens and cross bridges over the narrow streams of water. I avoid the beach and the ocean as I suspect most guests can be found there. I don't need anyone's company but my own.

And Blossom's. I force thoughts of her away. This obsession needs to end since it can't lead anywhere. She's not from

Smuggler's Hideaway. And she hasn't put down any roots here. She hasn't bought a house. Her only friends are her boss and Dakota. Mainlanders never stay on the island.

The bush beside me rustles before Alan appears. He's breathing hard as if he's been running. His mouth is moving but I can't hear him with my ear pods in. I pause my podcast and remove my ear pods.

"I'm sorry. Did you say something?"

Alan frowns at me. "You didn't hear me?"

Obviously not. "No."

He crosses his arms over his chest. "I don't believe you're married to Blossom."

Jumping straight to the matter at hand. Good. I abhor small talk. "Why not?"

He brandishes a hand at me. "Blossom would never marry a man like you."

A man like me? She didn't have any trouble chasing a man like me. I want to tell him as much but goading him won't help me figure out how he hurt her. And I'm determined to discover the truth.

"A man like me?"

"A nerd."

I push my glasses up my nose. "Are you making fun of me wearing glasses?"

His cheeks darken. "No."

"What makes you think I'm a nerd?" I am a nerd and I'm proud of it but I get the feeling he thinks nerd is a derogatory term.

"It doesn't matter. You're not Blossom's type."

I study Alan for a moment. He's several inches shorter than me and is thin to the point of being scrawny. Whereas I'm muscular from the time I spend rowing. I row for an hour most mornings before work.

I started rowing to keep an eye on Miles while he surfs. To my surprise, I enjoyed it. Nothing can compare to being out on the ocean while the sun rises before any of the tourists are on the beach. It's quiet. Unlike the rest of my life, which is filled with five brothers who talk nonstop. I can ignore them, but it's nice not to need to.

"Blossom's type isn't tall, fit men?"

He sneers. "Don't be an asshole."

If I were one of my younger brothers, I'd remind him he started this conversation. Instead, I nod and make to leave. He stands in my path to stop me.

"You won't get away with it."

"Get away with what?"

"Pretending to be married."

I sigh. "This again."

"I won't drop the lawsuit for this charade."

Finally, we're getting to the heart of the matter. "The lawsuit?"

He barks out a laugh. "This is precious. She didn't tell you."

I step closer to him. "Tell me what?"

"I thought you were married. You should know about the lawsuit if you're married." He smirks. "If you married her for her money, you're going to be sorely disappointed when I win this case."

Heat flushes through my body and I fist my hands at my hips before I deck him. This man deserves a broken nose, but I won't find out about this lawsuit if he's at the emergency room. And if I punch him, he will be at the emergency room.

"I didn't marry her for her money. I have my own money. I'm part owner of *Buccaneer's Whiskey*."

And my brother is a billionaire who thinks giving his brothers six-figure checks is a good way to make up for our dad abandoning us when we were kids. But Alan doesn't need to know about Eli. He's obviously money hungry. Eli has enough money-hungry people trying to wheedle their way into his life.

Alan's eyes narrow. "You're part owner of the local distillery?"

"And I'm the master distiller."

He rolls his eyes. "I understand Blossom's attraction now. She always was obsessed with distilling and brewing."

"Whatever," I mutter and try to leave again.

"But I still don't believe you're married."

"This is becoming tiresome."

"Blossom's a talker. She wouldn't hide her inheritance from her parents from the man she's married to."

Inheritance from her parents?

"She told me her parents have passed," I lie. She said she didn't have any family, which is not the same as telling me about their deaths.

"But she obviously didn't tell you they left her a boatload of money when they died."

No, she didn't. And I would have never guessed Blossom has money. She works sixty hours a week, lives in a shitty apartment building, and doesn't wear fancy clothes or jewelry.

"I bet that's how you can afford to stay in a chalet this weekend."

"I'm paying for the chalet." Blossom offered to pay for half but I refused her offer.

"I nearly forgot." He snaps his fingers as if he just thought of something. "She can't touch the money because of the lawsuit."

"I'm done with your riddles. Tell me whatever it is you want to tell me or let me be."

"Shouldn't you be with Blossom?"

"She's getting ready for the welcome lunch."

He groans. "Don't you hate how long she needs to get ready?"

"No, because the result is always worth it."

"She has you tied around her little finger."

She doesn't, but I wouldn't mind if she did.

"Are we done?"

I start to walk away.

"I'm not giving up until I get what I'm owed," he hollers after me, and I stop to listen. "We were married when she received the inheritance, which means half of the money is mine. She can pretend we weren't married and she's married to you all she wants. I will win this lawsuit."

"We're not pretending," I tell him before stalking toward our chalet.

The pieces of Blossom's past are starting to fall into place, but I'm still missing a few essential pieces. Was she married to Alan? Why does he think he deserves the money her parents left her?

I'm finding out the truth and then we'll figure out a way to stop Alan. Because that asshole is not getting any of Blossom's money.

Chapter 14

"What do you want to know?" ~ Blossom

Blossom

The door to the chalet opens. "I'm nearly ready." I glance at my watch. "Which gives us five minutes to walk to the main building. We'll be five minutes early." Which I consider to be on time.

When Jaxon doesn't reply, I set my lipstick on the vanity and make my way into the bedroom of the chalet, where he's pacing back and forth.

"We need to talk."

My heart lodges in my throat. "You changed your mind?"

He turns to face me and freezes. His gaze rakes over my body and his eyes heat. My nipples tighten in response.

"You…you…" He blows out a breath. "You look beautiful."

My cheeks warm. "Thank you."

He steps close and grasps my hand. "We need to talk."

Crap on a mermaid cracker. He did change his mind. He doesn't want to pretend to be my husband this weekend. Alan will realize I'm not married, and I'll lose the lawsuit. I can't lose the lawsuit. The inheritance is mine!

"Did you change your mind? Do you want to go into the hot tub after all?" I try to joke, but judging by the frown on Jaxon's face, I didn't succeed.

He leads me to the sofa and helps me to sit before sitting next to me. "I ran into Alan."

"Ugh. What did he say? Was he nasty?" I bury my face in my hands. I can imagine all the mean things my ex would say about me. All things I don't want Jaxon to know.

He tugs my hands away from my face. "He mentioned your parents, the inheritance, and the lawsuit."

I throw my head back and yell at the ceiling. "Is this my punishment for cheating on one physics test in college? I told the professor and re-took the exam. Which I nearly failed and it ruined my GPA. Haven't I been punished enough?"

Jaxon pinches my chin and forces me to meet his gaze. "What happened with Alan?"

"Don't you want to ask me about the physics exam?"

He snorts. "I have five brothers who are masters in avoiding the truth and changing the subject. You're going to have to try harder than this."

I slump my shoulders. "I had to ask a man with five hellraising brothers to be my fake husband."

"Why do you need a fake husband for this wedding? It's more than showing Alan you've leveled up. There's more to it."

I bite my bottom lip as I contemplate how to answer.

He tugs my lip free. "I know your parents died. I know there's an inheritance. I know Alan's suing you."

I grunt. "Alan has a big fat mouth."

"Alan's an asshole," he mutters.

"He wasn't always an asshole. When we met in college, he was fun. He wasn't a jokester or a prankster the way your brothers are, but we had fun together. We went to football games with painted buffalos on our face, crashed frat parties we weren't invited to, and enjoyed a ton of concerts."

"Buffalos?"

"University of Colorado Boulder is my alma mater."

"Good school."

"Did you think I went to a crummy school? Just because I'm not a nerd doesn't mean I'm stupid."

He chuckles. "You're trying to distract me again."

I blow him a raspberry. "You really won't let me distract you?"

"Nope."

I notice the time on the alarm clock next to the bed. "But we're going to be late for the welcome lunch."

"I don't give a shit. I'm not going to an event where I will most likely run into your asshole ex without knowing the full story. He already doesn't believe we're married."

My brow wrinkles. "He doesn't believe we're married? How do you know?"

"He told me. Several times."

Damn. If he doesn't believe we're married, he'll never drop the lawsuit. My face crumples and I fight to keep the tears forming in my eyes from falling. I will not cry in front of my fake husband.

Jaxon wraps an arm around my shoulders and pulls me near until I drop my head on his shoulder.

"I hate when you're hurting," he murmurs as he combs his fingers through my hair.

My heart thuds in my chest. No one's cared whether I'm hurting or not in a long time. I nearly forgot how it feels to be offered physical comfort. I nestle into his hold.

I know this is fake but I'm accepting the comfort anyway. No one said I wasn't allowed to have some benefits from this arrangement.

"I hate to hurt you more, but I have to know the truth. Alan will make our lives a living hell this weekend otherwise."

I push away to stare up at him. "Are you serious? You want to continue with this charade?" He nods. "But this isn't what you signed up for."

"I don't remember adding a clause to our agreement about backing out if things got tough."

"But…" I snap my mouth closed. Bringing up how he ran away and avoided me after our panty-melting kiss won't help anything.

I blow out a breath and gather my courage. "What do you want to know?"

"Everything, but I'll settle for why Alan's suing you."

Unfortunately, I can't explain why Alan is suing me without explaining everything.

"My parents were awesome." He cringes but I can't stop to ask him why. If I stop now, I'll never finish this story.

"Mom couldn't have any more children after me. So, Mom, Dad, and I were a tight-knit unit. I was never one of those kids who was embarrassed of my parents. Why would I be? They were awesome. Our house is where my friends congregated every day after school. Mom always had cookies for us, and Dad would come home with pizza at least once a week."

"Your childhood sounds magical."

I sigh. "It was."

I clear my throat and force myself to continue. "I didn't want to leave for college, but CU Boulder has an excellent chemical engineering department."

Jaxon fiddles with the ends of my hair. "And you met Alan at CU Boulder?"

I nod. "After graduation, he got a job in Boulder and I decided to stay there with him. I should have gone back home to Denver. I never should have stayed."

He squeezes my shoulder. "What happened?"

"My parents were coming to visit us two years ago for Christmas since Alan couldn't get any time off for the holidays. There was a snowstorm. A driver of a semi-truck lost control and slid into their lane. They didn't make it."

Jaxon doesn't hesitate. He gathers me into his arms and settles me on his lap. "Let it all out, Petal. Let it all out."

I cling to his t-shirt as the tears I was holding back break through. Jaxon rubs his hand up and down my back and murmurs to me until I manage to get myself under control.

"I'm sorry you lost them," he says.

"Me too," I whisper. "But there's more."

"Tell me, Petal."

"My parents left me a bit of money. When Alan found out, he contacted a contractor and had him draw up plans to expand our house. He didn't tell me. I found out when the workers showed up to start work."

Jaxon growls. "Are you fucking kidding me?"

"I asked him how we were going to pay for all the work. Our inheritance was his answer. *Our* inheritance. I wasn't planning on touching the money and he had already spent it. I walked out of the house and never came back. I was done."

"And now he's suing you for half of the money."

"Asshole," I mutter.

"But why does he think he's entitled to the money?"

"Because he's an asshole who claims we were married when I inherited the money."

"Wouldn't you know if you were married?"

"Colorado is a common law state. He claims we acted as husband and wife in public and therefore we were married."

"And so you told him you were already married," Jaxon guesses correctly.

"I didn't know what else to do. I never presented myself as his wife. Did I use his last name to make dinner reservations? Sure. But if I had wanted to marry him, we would have discussed marriage."

"You owned a home together, but you didn't want to marry him?"

I shrug. I'm not explaining to him how I ignored all the red flags. How I was a foolish girl who wanted to be loved.

"Do you think Alan will drop the lawsuit if he thinks you're married?"

"I'm hoping he will. I can't stand the idea of him getting any money from my parents. How dare he demand half! He didn't even attend their funeral because he had a 'work project'. Work project my ass." I snort. "Screwing your colleague isn't a work project."

Jaxon's nostrils flare. "He was with his lover while you were at your parents' funeral?"

"Yep. He denies it, but the used condoms in the waste basket proved him wrong."

"I should have decked him."

I blink. "What?"

"I wanted to punch him in the face but I held back. I shouldn't have."

"I hate to point this out because I would love to witness Alan getting married with a black eye, but violence isn't going to help him drop the lawsuit."

"Neither is pretending to be married," he mutters before lifting me off his lap.

My stomach rolls. "You don't want to pretend to be married this weekend after all?"

Sinking mermaids. Alan is never going to drop this lawsuit.

"Not what I said," he mutters as he digs his phone out. "Go wash your face. We don't have much time."

"Time for what?" I ask but he waves and walks out onto the deck without answering.

What is he doing?

Chapter 15

"Being a nerd doesn't mean I can't pull off a surprise." ~ Jaxon

JAXON

I wait until Blossom shuts the door to the bathroom behind her to connect the call.

"I thought you were at the wedding," Eli says when he answers.

"I need my brothers."

"We've been on standby all morning. I'll rally the troops and we'll be at the resort within the hour."

"Not the resort. I need to plan a wedding."

Silence falls.

"Eli, did you hear me?"

"I'm hallucinating. I'm trying to figure out what I did to piss Paisley off. She must have put hallucinogens in my coffee."

I growl. "This isn't the time for jokes."

"Jaxon, you haven't had a serious relationship since high school."

Technically, I've never had a serious relationship. It's difficult to have a serious relationship when you know she'll eventually leave you anyway. But this isn't about me. This is about Blossom. She needs me.

"Raider brother secret," I insist.

"By barnacle, booze, and brotherhood – what's said is sunk," he vows.

"Blossom's ex is suing her for her inheritance from her parents and she thinks he'll drop the suit if he believes we're married. Alan isn't buying we're married, so we're getting married."

"Does Blossom know she's getting married?"

"No, but she will. Can you set it up?"

"For today?"

I check my watch. "In an hour, preferably."

"When you call in a brother favor, you don't mess around."

"Can you do it or not?"

He snorts. "Of course, I can. Meet you at city hall at one-thirty."

I quickly hang up as Blossom is opening the sliding doors.

"Are you ready?" I ask.

"Are we going to the welcome lunch?" She checks the time and cringes. "We're thirty minutes late."

"We'll be back in time for the rehearsal dinner."

I usher her back into the chalet and toward the door. She doesn't fight me. Does she trust me after how I treated her after our kiss? My body warms – I want her to trust me – but I push those thoughts away. This isn't about me.

"Where are we going?" Blossom asks once we're settled in my car and driving toward Smuggler's Rest.

"It's a surprise."

"If you're trying to cheer me up after hearing my sad story, there's no need. It's sweet. But not necessary."

I reach across the console to squeeze her thigh. Her dress is thin, allowing me to feel the heat of her skin through the material. My cock wakes up. It wants to feel her thighs wrapped around my hips as I bury myself in her.

I realize I'm caressing her skin and snatch my hand back.

"It's completely necessary."

She rubs her hands together. "What are we going to do? I'm up for an adventure. The last time I went on one, Dakota ended up giving some stranger a bloody nose and it ruined our fun."

I chuckle. "She has a habit of giving people bloody noses."

She places her hand over her face. "I hope she doesn't give me one. My nose is one of my favorite features on my face."

I pull her hand away. "You should like all your features. You're beautiful."

She rolls her eyes. "There's no need to play husband now. We're alone. No one can hear you."

I squeeze her hand before releasing it. "No playing. You are beautiful."

"And here I thought Miles Raider was the smooth talker in the family."

"Trust me. He is. But Zane and Kai aren't far behind."

"Speaking of Zane, Kai, and Miles." She points to my brothers standing on the sidewalk outside of City Hall.

"We're here," I say and park in front of them.

"Here? Does this adventure involve all of the Raider brothers? I'm not into multiple sex partners. I admit I enjoy reading reverse harem novels, but I have no desire to try and have a harem of men. Especially not brothers."

My mouth gapes open. "What are you talking about?"

Her cheeks darken. "No reverse harem. Check."

Miles opens her door before I can get there. I shove him out of the way.

"Sorry. I should have let you open the door for your bride yourself."

"Bride?" Blossom asks. "We're only pretending to be married."

Miles holds up his hands as he retreats. "Oops."

Eli waves from the entrance to City Hall. "You've got five minutes."

Five minutes to explain to Blossom why we're getting married at City Hall? This is going to be interesting.

I shackle her wrist and drag her to the alley next to the building.

"Are you kidnapping me?" she asks as she studies the alley. "Is there a speakeasy I don't know about?" Her nose wrinkles. "I don't know if it's a good idea to get drunk before dealing with Alan. I might end up punching him."

I cradle her face between my hands and kiss her nose. "I'm not kidnapping you. We're getting married."

She gapes at me for a long moment before gulping. "Married?"

I nod. "Married. Alan doesn't believe we're married, but it doesn't matter what he believes if we actually are married."

"But this isn't fake, Jaxon. This is real. When you fall in love and want to get married." Pain lights up her eyes before she blinks and it disappears. "You'll have to tell your future wife you're divorced. I can't do that to you."

"You're not doing anything to me. This is my choice."

She scowls. "I can't let you make this choice."

"You're not letting me do anything. But you do have a choice. You can get your sexy ass into the courthouse and marry me, or you can continue to fight Alan over a lawsuit no judge should allow."

"Sexy ass."

My eyes fall closed. "That's all you heard?"

She shrugs. "A woman enjoys hearing she has a sexy ass. Especially from a man who ghosted her after he melted her panties with a kiss."

I rest my forehead against hers. "I'm sorry. I never should have ghosted you."

"Or called me a mistake."

"Or called you a mistake."

"Or pretended you were invisible."

"Or pretended I was invisible."

When she doesn't continue, I cock an eyebrow. "I'm done."

"Do you accept my apology?"

"You're marrying me to get my ex to drop a lawsuit. I think you're good."

I chuckle. This woman. Just when I think I know what she's going to say, she surprises me. She'd surprise me for the rest of my life if I let her. Too bad there is no rest of my life. This marriage won't be any more real than the marriage we pretended we were in this morning when we checked into the resort.

I step away before grasping her hand and leading her out of the alley. When we reach the sidewalk, my brothers cheer.

"She said yes!" Miles shouts.

"Yes, to bad sex with Jaxon for the rest of her life," Kai adds and they high-five each other.

Dakota pushes her way past my brothers to hand Blossom a bouquet. "I'm sorry it's not tulips. Jaxon said tulips but they're out of season and you have to order them in advance."

"You remembered my favorite flower?" Blossom asks me.

I roll my eyes. "Don't be flattered. I'm a genius."

She elbows me. "You remembered. You like me," she sings.

"Obviously, I like you. We're getting married."

"About getting married," Dakota begins.

I know, as Blossom's best friend, she must have questions, but when we're surrounded by my nosy brothers is not the proper time to discuss this.

"Not now," I tell her. "We have a wedding to attend."

Dakota nods before leaving us to stand with Rhett.

Eli whistles. "We need to go."

I offer Blossom my elbow. She hesitates. "Are you sure about this? You don't have to do this."

"I'm doing what I want to." She stares at me for a long moment before finally threading her arm through mine.

"I'm sorry," I say as we walk.

She rears back. "Sorry about what? Being a perfect gentleman? Riding in on a white horse to save me?"

"Technically, it wasn't a horse."

"A mustang is a horse."

I nod to acknowledge her point since I do drive a Mustang. "I'm sorry this isn't the perfect wedding you imagined. You have to wear shoes. There's no beach. And the flowers aren't your favorite."

"Jaxon Raider." She glares at me. "Don't you dare apologize for helping me out or I'll consult Paisley for a prank."

Paisley, standing next to Eli, clears her throat. "I am always available for consultations with a member of the sisterhood."

We arrive at the mayor's office, and Eli knocks. "Come in," Lana, the mayor of Smuggler's Rest, replies.

"Show time," Blossom whispers before Eli opens the door and we file into the office.

"A last-minute wedding," Lana cheers. Her gaze drops to Blossom's stomach. "And not a shotgun wedding. Love this!"

Lana is a bit of a romantic, which is probably why she's been married five times. She hurries around her desk to stand in front of us.

"The lovebirds stay here. Who are the witnesses?"

"Eli and Dakota."

Blossom mock glares at me. "Stop being perfect."

"I want to make you happy. This one's easy."

"That's what she said," Miles mutters behind me. Rhett smacks him upside the head. I nod at Rhett in thanks.

"Dakota, you come stand next to Blossom. Eli, you stand next to Jaxon." Once everyone has rearranged themselves, she asks, "Who has the rings?"

"We don't have rings," Blossom says at the same time Eli says, "I do."

"It appears we're ready," Lana says. "Jaxon and Blossom, are you ready to proclaim the foundation of love for one another in the sight of these witnesses and all the smugglers and mermaids who have gone before you?"

I lift an eyebrow at Blossom, and she nods. "We are."

"Jaxon Raider, do you take Blossom Nelson to be your lawfully wedded partner – your lobster in the trap of life, your moonshine mule, your co-captain on this possibly doomed but definitely entertaining voyage?

Will you promise to love her even when she steals the blankets, honor her even when she forgets to do the dishes, trust her the way a smuggler trusts low tide, and commit to her with the same reckless devotion you'd give to a bottomless jar of Smuggler's Hideaway moonshine?

Will you stand by her side through smooth sailing, ship-wrecks, suspicious mermaid sightings, and family dinners with the full crew – until death or a very dramatic sea curse do you part?"

I meet Blossom's gaze. Her burnished whiskey colored eyes are filled with wonder and a bit of mirth. I want to witness this look in her eyes every day for the rest of my days.

This is fake, Jaxon, I remind myself.

"I do."

"Blossom Nelson, do you take Jaxon Raider to be your lawfully wedded partner – your lobster in the trap of life, your moonshine mule, your co-captain on this possibly doomed but definitely entertaining voyage?

Will you promise to love him even when he steals the blankets, honor him even when he forgets to do the dishes, trust him the way a smuggler trusts low tide, and commit to him with the same reckless devotion you'd give to a bottomless jar of Smuggler's Hideaway moonshine?

Will you stand by his side through smooth sailing, ship-wrecks, suspicious mermaid sightings, and family dinners with the full crew – until death or a very dramatic sea curse do you part?"

She smiles at me. "I do."

Lana beams at us. She is absolutely loving this. "At this time, Jaxon and Blossom will exchange rings. The wedding ring is a symbol of binding. A symbol of attachment and of belonging, not of possession, but of partnership."

Eli digs the rings out of his pocket and hands one to me.

"Have you written your own vows?" Lana asks.

"I'll wing it," I say.

She nods and motions for me to proceed. I take Blossom's left hand and notch the ring on her ring finger. Her eyes widen and she retreats.

"That diamond is massive. I'm not wearing it."

I catch her before she manages to escape out the door. "Do you want Alan to drop the lawsuit or not?"

"Shush," she hisses as she glances around at everyone who is undoubtedly trying to eavesdrop. "Does everyone know?"

"I had to tell Eli to get this arranged, but he swore on barnacles and booze and brotherhood not to tell."

"No one else knows?"

I shake my head. "No one else knows."

She blows out a breath. "Okay. I'll wear the ring this weekend but that's my final offer."

I lead her back to our place in front of Lana. This time, when I place the ring on Blossom's finger, she doesn't balk.

"I promise to stand beside you – through calm seas, stormy nights, and small-town gossip. I vow to keep your secrets, laugh at your jokes even when I don't understand them, and pretend not to notice when you sip the whiskey from my glass. I'll be your partner in public and... your problem in private."

Blossom holds out her hand to Eli and he drops the match of Blossom's ring into her palm.

She poises the ring at the tip of my finger. "I promise to stand beside you – even when you pretend you're invisible. I promise to laugh at your nerdy t-shirts and not notice when you forget to put the toilet seat down. I'll be your problem in public and your partner in private."

She pushes the ring onto my finger. I thought it would feel awkward, but the gold feels natural on my finger as if it was always meant to be there.

"By the power vested in me by the town of Smuggler's Hideaway, I now declare you husband and wife. You may kiss."

I lean over and meet Blossom's lips. It's meant to be a quick and sweet kiss. But the second I taste her cherry lips, I can't help myself from deepening the kiss. From sweeping my tongue into her mouth for more. I wrap my arms around her.

Eli claps me on the back and I stumble backward. Shit. We're not alone.

I glance at Blossom. Her lips are swollen, her cheeks are flushed, and her brown eyes have darkened to polished mahogany. She's the most beautiful woman I've ever seen.

I want to keep her.

Chapter 16

"I need to forget my clothes more often." ~ Blossom

Blossom

I stare at the diamond ring on my finger as we drive back to the resort after our quickie wedding. The diamond is huge, but it's not ostentatious. It's classy and beautiful. And not mine to keep, I remind myself.

"You only have to wear it this weekend," Jaxon says. "Once Alan drops the lawsuit, you can drop the ring."

"And we'll get our marriage annulled."

"It should be a simple procedure."

My stomach drops at his quick agreement. I should want an annulment. I hardly know Jaxon. We've shared a mere two kisses. But I don't want to annul our marriage.

I should want to. I've learned my lesson with men. But Jaxon is the complete opposite of Alan.

"The ring is pretty," I say, since I don't want to discuss our annulment any longer.

Jaxon grins. "I'm glad you like it."

I check the time on my phone. "We missed the welcome lunch and the wine tasting this afternoon, but we should make the rehearsal dinner. It's two hours from now."

He lifts his eyebrow. "Should make it? We're five minutes from the resort. How much time do you need to get ready?"

"I have to change outfits. And I have to wash my hair."

"Wash your hair? It looks lovely."

I wiggle my eyebrows at him. "But it'll probably get wet in the hot tub."

He shakes his head. "I should have known."

We arrive at the resort and he hurries around the car to open my door. He takes my bouquet from me before offering me his hand. "I'm glad you kept the bouquet."

"It's too pretty to sit in my apartment while I'm away for the weekend." And it's the first flowers Jaxon gave to me. I want them near me.

We skip the building with the reception and walk to the gardens where our chalet is. I notice a group of tables set up near the beach. I point to it. "It must be the wine tasting."

"Do you want to go?"

My nose wrinkles. "Do I want to drink wine with a bunch of pretentious people?"

"You don't know they're pretentious."

I giggle. "Trust me. Alan is all about impressing people. Like attracts like."

"Blossom!" Alan shouts.

I pretend I don't hear him.

"Blossom!" he shouts again and waves at us.

I wave back. "Hello!"

"Come join us for wine!"

"I can't hear you. The wind." I cup my ear with my hand and shrug as if I'm oh so disappointed to not be able to hear whatever my asshole ex-boyfriend is saying. I might be enjoying this a bit too much.

Alan starts jogging toward us.

Jaxon chuckles. "You handled the situation well."

I ignore him and begin speed walking toward our chalet. He hurries to keep up with me.

"He's following us. He's speeding up."

I glance around for somewhere to hide. There are no buildings nearby. Just trees and plants. And there – a hedge.

I jump over the hedge, pulling Jaxon with me. I lay flat on the ground. Jaxon opens his mouth to speak but I slap a hand over his mouth. "Quiet," I hiss.

"Blossom! Blossom!" Alan yells as he runs past.

I wait a few minutes after he passes before kneeling and peeking over the hedge. Alan's nowhere to be seen.

"Phew. He's gone."

"One thing you were right about," Jaxon says.

"What?"

He pulls a twig out of my hair. "You need to wash your hair."

I slap his shoulder. "It's not my fault they're doing the wine tasting next to reception. I would have walked around if I'd known."

He stands and pulls me to my feet. "I'm glad I discovered my wife enjoys playing dirty."

I roll my eyes. "Whatever."

"Want to get in the hot tub with me?" I ask when we arrive at the chalet.

His blue eyes darken but he shakes his head. "Nah. I want to finish listening to my podcast."

"You can listen to your podcast in the hot tub. I won't mind." It'd give me the chance to study his naked chest and shoulders without him realizing it.

His nose wrinkles. "I'm not much for hot tubs. I'll go for a walk."

My stomach sinks as he shuts the door behind him. I was looking forward to spending some time with my husband. But he couldn't escape fast enough.

It's a good reminder – this marriage is fake. Despite the massive diamond ring. And the beautiful flowers.

Fake, Blossom. Fake. Fake. Fake.

Jaxon hasn't returned by the time I drag myself out of the hot tub and into the shower. I'm drying my hair in my bra and panties when I realize I didn't bring my dress into the bathroom. I set the hairdryer down on the vanity.

"Jaxon!" When he doesn't respond, I slowly open the door. "Jaxon!"

I peek into the bedroom. When I ascertain it's empty, I rush to the closet where I hung up my dresses earlier. I grab the dress for tonight and whirl around.

I freeze when I realize Jaxon is standing rooted to a spot at the door. "Sorry. I … um… forgot my dress."

His gaze rakes over me from top to toe. My body vibrates with excitement in response. It urges me to cross the space between us and jump Jaxon.

I'm tempted. Severely tempted. But this man ignored me for weeks after we kissed. I can't risk his rejection. Certainly not now, when I know how kind and sweet he is. What a gentleman he is. His kind rejection would kill me.

"I'll just…" I rush across the room to the bathroom. I slam the door behind me and lean against it as I inhale large gulps of air.

I bet sex with Jaxon would be intense, considering the way he gets hyper focused. I want his attention focused on me. While we're both naked. And sweaty.

My alarm beeps to let me know we need to leave in five minutes and I shove away from the door. There's no time to dream about sex with the hot nerd now.

"You clean up nice," I tell Jaxon as we walk to the rehearsal dinner.

He's wearing a suit and tie. The suit must be custom made since it fits his broad shoulders and narrow waist perfectly. The tie matches his blue eyes. He's sexy in his nerdy t-shirts and jeans but in a suit? He's nearly irresistible.

He tugs at the knot of the tie at his neck. "I don't understand how Eli wears a tie every day. It's uncomfortable."

"I suppose you get used to it. The way women get used to high heels."

His gaze drops to my feet and his eyes heat. "I've never seen you in high heels before."

"Don't get used to it, mister. These heels are strictly for emergencies."

He chuckles. "Your definition of emergency is incorrect."

I giggle. "There can be more than one correct definition."

He rolls his eyes before opening the door to the main building of the resort which houses the restaurant, event space, and the indoor swimming pool.

He places a hand on my lower back to guide me through the hallway and I shiver. He has big hands. I bet they're big, capable hands that know how to satisfy a woman.

Alan appears at the end of the hallway and all thoughts of sex fly out of my mind. My ex was not a master with big, capable hands.

"You made it."

Way to state the obvious. "We're here."

His eyes narrow. "As opposed to the welcome lunch and wine tasting."

I'm hardly going to tell him the truth – we were off having a quickie marriage. I glance up at Jaxon from beneath my eyelashes instead. "We had more important things to do."

Jaxon wraps an arm around my shoulder and hauls me close. "The hot tub was a very important thing to do."

Alan narrows his eyes as he studies us. "Hot tub? Ms. Vanilla in a hot tub?"

Asshole. How dare he call me Ms. Vanilla? He's the one who always wanted sex on a schedule. Probably because he needed to fit in sex with his girlfriend in between sex with his mistress.

Jaxon smirks. "It was a very enjoyable afternoon."

I pat his chest. "Because I was with you."

He lifts my hand and kisses my palm. "And I was with you, wife."

"If you're trying to convince me you're married, I'm not buying it," Alan growls.

"You don't have to buy it. Facts are facts. They're either true or they're disproven," Jaxon says.

Alan rolls his eyes. "Such a nerd."

I bite my bottom lip as I stare at Jaxon. "Turns out I have a thing for nerds. Especially when they wear glasses and cheesy t-shirts."

"Hey!" Jaxon frowns. "I thought you liked my t-shirts."

"I like them better when they're on the bedroom floor." I wink.

He grins as he toys with my ring. "And I enjoy it when—"

"What the hell?" Alan's screech cuts Jaxon off. "She's wearing your ring?"

I hold out my hand and wag it in front of Alan's face. "Isn't it pretty?"

"But you hate rings."

Jaxon puffs out his chest. "I made it worth her while to wear mine."

"You two are disgusting. I'm going to prove you're not married and then you'll drop this charade." Alan spins on his heel and stomps off.

He's going to be mighty surprised when he discovers we are married. And then he'll drop the lawsuit and Jaxon can stop pretending to be in love with me.

My stomach clenches. I don't want Jaxon to stop pretending. He's sweet and sexy and everything I've always wanted in a man.

And this is fake, I remind myself.

Chapter 17

"No, I don't want to dance." ~ Jaxon

JAXON

"Are you okay?" Blossom whispers as we make our way to our assigned table for the rehearsal dinner.

I realize I'm clinging to her hand and force myself to loosen my hold.

"I'm okay." She lifts her eyebrow, and I blow out a breath. "I'm not great with big groups of people."

She squeezes my arm. "I know. We don't have to stay long. Eat, boring speeches, and we're out of here. The prohibition officers will never catch us."

"For someone who didn't grow up on Smuggler's Hideaway, you've certainly adjusted quite well."

She shrugs. "I love it here. No one makes me feel as if I don't belong."

But how long will she love it here? When will she get bored and leave? I shove those thoughts away. The answers don't matter. This marriage is a charade.

I pull out her chair for her. "I'm glad you're here," I whisper in her ear before kissing her neck.

She shivers and my cock twitches. It wants to make her shiver a lot more. This is just for show, I remind it.

I feel eyes on me and scan the room. Alan is sitting at the sweetheart table throwing daggers at me with his eyes. I smile and wave. If he thinks he can intimidate me with a look, he's obviously never met my brothers. He's lucky I only pull pranks for the prank war with them.

I've barely had a chance to sit down when the food is served. Roast beef with au gratin potatoes, glazed carrots, and green beans with fried shallots.

Blossom rolls her eyes at the food. I lean in close. "Do you want me to order you something else?"

She snorts. "And give Alan the satisfaction? No way. He knows I hate roast beef."

I glance over my shoulder and, sure enough, Alan is watching us. He's obsessed with Blossom and I don't like it one bit. I wave at him with my left hand, showcasing my wedding ring. She's mine, asshole. When his eyes narrow, I know he got my message.

Blossom slathers her meat with the white sauce before slicing into it. "He thinks I won't eat it and he can complain yet again about how I waste money. I'll show him wasting money."

She shoves a large piece into her mouth, barely chews before swallowing it.

"It's a good thing—"

"Achoo!" Her sneeze cuts me off.

"Bless you."

"Achoo! Achoo! Achoo!"

I hand her a napkin for her nose. "Are you okay?"

"What's in… Achoo!...the white sauce? Achoo!"

I try the sauce. "Sour cream and…" I taste it again. "I believe it's horseradish."

"Oh no." Her eyes widen. The tip of her nose is red and shiny and her eyes are watering. "Horseradish makes me sneeze."

I transfer her roast beef to my plate. "I'll finish it. Do you want my po…?"

I trail off when she scoops up my potatoes and puts them on her plate. She shoves a forkful into her mouth. "What?" she asks when she notices me staring.

"Are you going to steal potatoes from my plate for the rest of our marriage?"

She nods as she chews. "If they have cheese in them."

"And here I thought I only had to guard my chocolate."

"Oh please. You wouldn't dare guard your chocolate."

"Maybe I would."

"It's cute you think I wouldn't find a way to steal your chocolate."

I notice Alan and his fiancée begin making their rounds. I'm not surprised when they make their way to our table first. I wait until he's within hearing range before I respond to Blossom.

"I'd have to punish you for stealing my chocolate."

Her eyes flare until the light brown is the color of a dark sherry. I'm fascinated by the way her eyes change colors. I want to watch them as I sink deep into her. What color will her eyes darken to then?

"You're not spanking me again," she breathes out.

"Why not? I seem to remember you enjoying it."

She gasps. "I did not!"

"Ahem!" Alan clears his throat. I contemplate ignoring him. I'm having way too much fun with Blossom.

It's a ruse, I remind myself. Merely a ruse.

I grasp Blossom's hand and we turn together to face Alan and his fiancée.

"Alan," Blossom greets with a flat voice. I bite my tongue before I chuckle at her cheekiness. This woman could keep me on my toes for the rest of my life. Too bad she won't.

"Alan," his fiancée elbows him when he doesn't speak. "Introduce me to your friends."

Judging by the hate in her eyes when she looks at Blossom, she knows exactly who we are. And isn't happy we're at her wedding. I can't blame her. I would have been pissed if Alan attended our ceremony.

"Of course, darling. Blossom, Jaxon, this is my fiancée, Stacey."

Blossom waves to Stacey, whose eyes widen when they catch on the ring. "That's some ring."

Blossom sighs as she studies the ring. "You think so?"

"It must have cost a pretty penny."

Blossom shrugs. "I don't care if it came from a box of cereal. I love it because Jaxon gave it to me."

I kiss her nose. "Anything for you, Petal."

"Glad you could tear yourselves away from the hot tub to attend one of the wedding activities," Alan says.

Stacey scowls. "Your room has a hot tub?"

"We're in a chalet," I tell her.

"But Alan said he couldn't get a discount for the chalet."

I fiddle with Blossom's ring. "My wife and I are still in our honeymoon stage. I wanted to spoil her."

Blossom giggles. "He means he wanted to watch me walk around in my bikini."

"Don't lie and say you don't enjoy strutting around in your bikini for me."

She smirks. "Of course, I do. I especially enjoy it when I throw my bikini top at you and you chase me."

A vision of Blossom standing in our chalet in her white lacy bra and matching panties flashes into my mind. What I wouldn't give to have seen her without her bra on. My cock twitches in agreement.

Alan clears his throat. "Speaking of chases."

I force my gaze away from Blossom. "Yes?"

"Why did you two run from me this afternoon?"

Blossom's brow wrinkles. "Run from you?"

"I waved at you. You waved back. When I started for you, you ran."

"I don't remember you starting for us." She meets my gaze. "But I do remember running."

I tug on her hair. "I always catch you."

She smiles and it lights up her face. "Yes, you do."

"Alan." Stacey jerks on his arm. "Let's greet our other guests."

"Of course."

They march off but not before I hear her mutter to him. "They're obviously married. How are we going to win this lawsuit now?"

"Damn." Blossom blows out a breath. "It doesn't sound as if they're giving up."

I rub her neck. "Don't worry. He'll drop the lawsuit eventually. The lawyer fees must cost a pretty penny."

"Not to mention how expensive this wedding is," she adds.

"What does he do for work?"

"He's a tire salesman."

My eyes widen. "I didn't realize tire salesmen earned enough money for a destination wedding."

Her nose wrinkles. "They don't."

I open my mouth to ask her more questions but the lights lower and music blares from the speakers. I wince but Blossom jumps to her feet.

"Let's dance!"

I hold up my hands. "I don't dance."

"Come on. It's *Gangnam Style*. Everyone knows this dance."

"I don't."

She grabs my hand and drags me out of my chair. "I'll teach you."

I debate fighting her but she's happy. After all the worry about Alan and the lawsuit, she deserves a bit of fun. I give in and allow her to pull me to the dance floor.

I'm afraid I'd allow her to pull me anywhere she wants.

Chapter 18

"You won't hear me complaining about lying in the bed I made." ~ Blossom

BLOSSOM

"I've never met someone who has absolutely zero sense of rhythm before," I tease as we walk back to the chalet after the rehearsal dinner and dance.

"I have rhythm," Jaxon argues.

"You stepped on my foot twice."

"I will accept credit for the first time, but the second time was your fault."

I lift a brow. "It's my fault you stepped on my foot?"

"You stopped dancing because you were laughing so hard."

"Because you tripped over your own feet and ended up grabbing the ass of the person dancing next to you. You're lucky his boyfriend found the situation hilarious."

He grunts. "I don't have time for dancing."

"You need to make time for having fun."

"I have fun," he growls and I shiver. What I wouldn't do to hear him growl while he's in bed with me.

"Are you cold?" He doesn't wait for an answer before un-buttoning his jacket and shrugging it off. "Here." He lays the jacket over my shoulders before wrapping an arm around my waist and pulling me near.

The jacket smells of him. Whiskey and ocean. The com-bination is surprising and intoxicating. I may steal this jacket before the weekend's over.

"Here we are." Jaxon ushers me into the chalet. "Do you want to shower to warm up?"

"I'll be fine. I don't like to shower before bed."

He steers me toward the bathroom. "You can get ready for bed first."

I slip his jacket off and hand it to him. "I should probably get my pajamas from my suitcase first. Before I end up running around the chalet in my underwear again."

His breath hitches. Does he want to watch me walk around the chalet in my panties and bra as much as I want to parade around in front of him? My nipples pebble at the idea of him feasting his gaze on me.

He steps back and motions to the closet. "Probably a good idea."

Disappointment rolls through me but I ignore it. This is a fake marriage. It's not real. We're not going to enjoy each other all night long. No matter how much I want to.

Jaxon is merely playing by the rules. He's not deliberately hurting me or playing games.

I find my nightshirt and hurry back to the bathroom. I dump the shirt on the vanity. I'm reaching for the door to shut it when

I realize I have a problem. There's no way I can get out of this dress without help. At least not without straining my back.

I peek into the bedroom. Jaxon is sitting on the bed with his face in his hands. Is something wrong? Does he regret marrying me? This arrangement?

"Jaxon," I call. His head whips up. "Can you unzip me?"

He stands and prowls toward me. There's no regret in his gaze. Only heat in those blue eyes as he comes closer.

"I've been wondering how you zipped up your dress all night."

I whirl around and lift my hair off my neck. "Sorry. It's a trade secret."

He slowly lowers my zipper. I feel the air hit my heated skin. I want to feel Jaxon stroke my naked back. But he doesn't touch me.

"There."

I grasp the front of my dress before it pools at my feet. As much as I enjoy the idea of flashing Jaxon, he doesn't want the same things I do.

He kisses my neck before stepping away and shutting the door.

I allow myself to enjoy the feel of his lips on my skin for a moment before shaking myself and getting into gear. I rush through my skin care regimen before piling my hair on top of my head.

I debate keeping my bra on – my nightshirt is old and threadbare – but I can't sleep when I'm uncomfortable. I shed my bra and slip into my nightshirt. It's long enough to cover my ass but not much longer.

I study myself in the mirror. I'm not a vision of sexiness. What was I thinking when I packed? I should have included a sexy negligee. Except I don't own one.

Oh well. Here goes nothing.

"The bathroom's all yours."

Jaxon's eyes heat as he stares at me. But then he blinks and it's gone. "I won't be a minute."

I climb into bed and switch on the television. I make myself comfortable as I flip through the channels.

Jaxon exits the bathroom and I can't help myself from watching as he walks around the chalet, making sure the doors are locked and the lights are switched off. When he finishes, he grabs two pillows from the bed.

"What are you doing?"

"I need a pillow to sleep."

"Which begs the question – why are you removing the pillows from the bed?"

"I'm not sleeping in the bed with you."

"Why not?" I narrow my eyes. "You don't still think I have cooties, do you?"

He grunts. "Cooties don't exist."

I slap the mattress next to me. "Then, get your butt in bed."

He sighs. "I don't think it's a good idea."

"Are you afraid I'm going to attack you in the middle of the night?"

He snorts. "As if I couldn't handle you."

"You're out of excuses, nerd boy."

"I'm not a boy," he growls and my stomach quivers. I am extremely aware he's not a boy.

I point to his t-shirt. "But you are a nerd." It says *I may be N Er Dy but only periodically.*

His cheeks darken. It's adorable. And sexy. Everything Jaxon does is sexy.

"I never denied being a nerd."

I love how he owns his nerdiness. Owns who he is. He's genuine. Unlike a certain man who's getting married tomorrow.

"Get in the bed, nerd."

He frowns. "I don't think it's a good idea."

I lift my hand in the Girl Scout salute. "I solemnly swear to not take advantage of you." I drop my hand. "Happy?"

"Were you ever a Girl Scout?"

"Brownie." I shrug. "Same thing." Except I got kicked out of the brownies for an unfortunate incident with a spider. I maintain it was an accident.

"What if I take advantage of you?"

I wish he would. My panties dampen as I imagine all the ways he could take advantage of me. Starting with touching my skin and ending with filling me with his cock. If I ask him, is it taking advantage?

I open my mouth to ask but snap it shut again when memories of how he ignored me for more than a month after our first kiss assail me. Jaxon is not a man who's interested in me. He's helping me out. End of discussion.

"I know judo. You don't have a chance."

He cocks an eyebrow. "Do you seriously know judo?"

I shrug. "I saw a documentary about the sport once."

"You saw a documentary about judo?"

"My remote was broken and I was too lazy to get up and change the channel."

He chuckles. "That, I believe."

I narrow my eyes on him. "But you can't believe I'd know judo?"

"You're extremely competitive. If you knew judo, you'd have a black belt and everyone on the island would know about it."

My nose wrinkles. "The people on the island are pretty nosy."

"Not what I meant and you know it."

I realize I'm digging my own grave and throw away the shovel. "Get in the bed. You're about two feet too tall for the sofa and there's no way I'm allowing you to sleep on the floor."

"Allowing me?"

"You heard me. Get your butt in the bed before I message your brothers that you're afraid to consummate this marriage."

"You have no idea the chaos my brothers would cause," he mutters but he does climb into bed.

I enjoy the look of him in my bed wearing his nerdy t-shirt and a pair of sweat shorts. I'd enjoy it even more if he removed his t-shirt. And his shorts. And his underwear.

Okay, fine. I want Jaxon naked in my bed. It's no surprise. I've longed for him since the moment he swooped his tongue into my mouth and shoved his hard length against my stomach.

Is his cock really as long and wide as it felt? Inquiring minds want to know. It's me. I'm the inquiring mind.

"What the hell are you watching?" he asks and I realize while I'm drooling over him and trying to figure out a way to get him to strip, he's glaring at the television.

Good reminder. This is fake, Blossom. F. A. K. E. Fake.

"It's *Storage Wars.*"

"Never heard of it."

I gasp. "You've never heard of *Storage Wars.* Have you been living in a barn?"

He motions to the television. "What's it about?"

"People bid for abandoned storage lockers. Then, they compete for who can earn the most money from whatever's in the locker."

"And you enjoy watching this?"

"Except for the whole guessing how much the stuff in the locker is worth. I think those numbers are highly inflated and complete bullshit."

"Give me an example." He props two pillows behind his back and makes himself comfortable.

I have a vision of us doing this every night. Before getting naked and enjoying each other. A longing hits me with such force, I have to blow out a breath before I jump Jaxon.

I haven't had a family in years. When my parents died, I thought I could build a family with Alan. But those dreams crumbled the second he thought he had rights to my inheritance.

Jaxon would never attempt to steal my money. For one, he doesn't need it. Besides, money isn't important to him. He's already loaded. All the owners of *Buccaneer's Whiskey & Distillery* are millionaires. But he wears t-shirts and old jeans while driving around in a Mustang that's seen better days.

If only he hadn't ghosted me after our first kiss.

Chapter 19

"I can't deny this woman anything." ~ Jaxon

JAXON

Blossom sighs and I glance over to find her fast asleep. I pry the remote control from her hands. She mutters something unintelligible in her sleep before rolling to the side. Her shirt hitches up, giving me a glimpse of her white undies.

My cock twitches. It urges me to pull those undies down.

Fuck. It's going to be a long night avoiding the temptation of Blossom. But I need to resist her.

Blossom isn't the woman for me. She's outgoing and loud and fun. I'm an introvert who's perfectly fine staying at home every Friday night. She would never be content with me or Smuggler's Hideaway. Not in the long run.

I switch off the television and the lights. I might as well get comfortable for this long night of torture.

Blossom's moan wakes me. Why is she moaning? Is she...

Crap. I'm wrapped around her with my hand on her breast.

I snatch my hand away. "I'm sorry. I didn't mean to…" I trail off when she rubs her ass against my cock. Damn. That feels good.

"Don't apologize. Finish what you started."

"It's not a good idea."

"Why not?" She rubs her ass against my hard cock again. "Afraid you can't please me?"

"Don't taunt me."

"Don't tease me."

"I didn't tease you on purpose. It was an accident."

She giggles. "It was an accident?"

"I was sleeping. I didn't realize what I was doing."

"And what's your excuse for rubbing yourself against my ass now?"

Shit. She's right. I am pressing my cock against her. I start to scoot away but she grabs my ass to keep me in place.

"You got me all hot and bothered. You can't leave me hanging now."

"This isn't a good idea," I repeat.

"I agree. It's not a good idea. It's a fantastic idea."

"Blossom," I growl.

"Jaxon," she growls back.

She rolls over to face me. Her t-shirt hitches up giving me a tantalizing view of the skin above her pretty white panties. My cock presses against my underwear, determined to reach her.

"Listen." Blossom places a hand on my chest and I nearly jump from the zap of electricity I feel at her touch. How would it feel to have her touch my naked skin?

"This doesn't have to mean anything. I want you. You want me. It doesn't have to be complicated."

"A one-night stand?"

She nods. "We are married after all."

"I don't want to hurt you."

"Hurt me? Are you into sadism? Do you want to cause me pain?"

I scowl. "Not what I meant and you know it."

"Jaxon, I'm a big girl. I can have a one-night stand and not get hurt."

But I'm not certain I can.

"Please, Jaxon," she pleads. "I want to think about something else than my ex getting married tomorrow while still fighting me for my inheritance."

Damn it. I don't want her lying here thinking about her ex.

"One time," I grumble.

"But I can have more than one orgasm, right?"

I growl. "You'll have more than one orgasm."

"Yippee!" she cheers.

"On your back," I demand.

She hurries to comply and I shove the covers off of the bed. There's enough moonlight shining in from the windows to notice how shiny her skin is.

"Are you going to be good for me?" She wiggles. "Stay still."

"Will staying still give me orgasms?"

"*I'll* be the one giving you orgasms tonight."

"Go ahead. Proceed. Let's get this party started."

"Impatient?"

She shrugs. "I haven't had an orgasm I haven't caused myself in a long time."

A vision of her pleasuring herself jumps into my mind and my cock pulses in response. I grit my teeth before I forget all about preparing her and rip her panties off.

I glide my hands along the smooth skin of her legs until I touch her panties. I skate my fingertips along the edge of the lace. Goosebumps form in my wake and she moans. If she's this affected by my finger grazing her skin, how will she respond when I dive into her?

I can't wait to find out.

I get to my knees and whip off my t-shirt. Blossom immediately reaches for me but I shackle her hands to stop her.

"Your turn." I nod to her shirt.

"I can't take my shirt off without hands."

I lift her hands above her head. "Grab the headboard."

"Make it worth my while, nerd boy."

"Man," I correct.

I wait until she grasps the headboard before grabbing the hem of her t-shirt. The material bunches as I lift it up her body revealing her naked breasts.

I can't resist. I lean forward and latch onto a nipple. Blossom arches her back, shoving her chest into my face. It's an offer I can't refuse.

I nip and suck on her nipple until it's a hard point. Until she wraps her legs around my waist and begins rubbing herself on my hard cock.

I release her nipple with a pop before moving onto the other one. I nibble on the hard point and she moans.

"Jaxon."

I love hearing her say my name in a breathy voice. I wonder if I can get her to scream my name.

Time to find out.

I sit up. Her t-shirt is bunched up under her neck. Her face is flushed. And her eyes are glazed over. Next time, I'll keep the light on so I can see what color her eyes turn when she's overcome with passion.

Except. There won't be a next time. This is my one chance to taste and touch her. I shouldn't waste it.

"Lift your arms." I whip her t-shirt off and throw it behind me.

I pause to admire how beautiful she is. What I wouldn't do to have this woman naked in my bed every night. But it's not to be. She would never stay with me.

"Snap a picture. It'll last longer."

"Let me grab my phone." I pretend to reach for my phone.

She squeals. "It was a joke. It was a joke."

I smirk. "I know."

She slaps my shoulder. "Not funny, nerd man."

"I thought it was funny."

"Jaxon has jokes. Miracles never cease."

Her smile lights up her face and I can't resist. I dip my head and press my lips to hers. She sighs and I slip my tongue inside. Her cherry taste hits me and I groan. I fucking love cherries.

I explore her mouth until she clutches my shoulders and digs her fingernails into my skin. Her legs wrap around my waist and she rubs herself against my cock. My cock doesn't understand why we're not buried deep inside her heat now.

I snake my hand between our bodies and slip my hand under her panties. She drops her legs from around my waist and widens for me.

"Good girl," I mumble against her lips.

I bypass her clit and plunge two fingers into her wet pussy. Her walls tighten around me.

"You like that?"

"Mmm…"

I still. "I asked a question."

Her eyes fly open and she glares at me. "I don't like it when you stop."

"Not the question I asked."

"You become a chatty Cathy in bed."

I slowly withdraw my fingers. "I can stop."

"No. No. No."

I raise my eyebrow and wait for her to respond.

"Yes. I like it when you touch me. Satisfied?"

I smirk. "Not yet. But you will be soon."

"Yes, please."

"I like it when you're polite."

"Don't get…" Her voice trails off when I begin pumping my fingers in her.

Her inner walls tighten around me. "Are you going to come for me, Petal?"

"Yes," she breathes out.

I rub my palm against her clit as I continue to thrust into her pussy. Her legs tremble and her walls convulse. She's nearly there. She plants her heels onto the bed and meets me thrust for thrust.

"Come," I whisper in her ear. "Come for me."

Her mouth falls open in a silent scream and her walls tighten around me as she climaxes.

"Yes. Yes. Yes." She chants as I draw out her orgasm with my fingers.

Only when she collapses on the bed, do I withdraw my fingers. I scramble to my knees.

"My turn." I pull her panties down her legs before pushing my shorts and boxers down. I reach for her but stop. "Shit."

"What's wrong?"

"Condom." I didn't bring any with me. I didn't want to assume.

"In the drawer."

My brow furrows. "Did you bring condoms?" Did she plan this? Did she want to seduce me?

"Nope. According to the note, the resort provides condoms for all its guests. In fact, you can ask for more 'adult toys' if need be."

"Adult toys?" Blossom would be beautiful tied to the four-poster bed. I shake those thoughts away. No time now. And this is one time only. No repeats.

I snatch a condom from the drawer. Once it's on, I settle between Blossom's thighs and notch my cock at her entrance.

"You sure about this?"

"You going to give me another orgasm?"

"Maybe more than one," I grumble.

She smiles and the sight hits me straight in the heart. How I wish I could see her smile in my bed every day for the rest of my life. But it's not to be.

I sink into her. Fuck. She feels amazing. Better than anyone before her. I fear better than anyone after her.

I push those thoughts away. Now is not the time to worry about the future. Not when I have the woman I'm obsessed with naked and writhing beneath me.

Chapter 20

BLOSSOM

The sun shines in my face and I groan. Ugh. I forgot to close the curtains again.

I open one eye a smidgeon and a view of a deck with the ocean beyond it greets me. What the hell? This isn't my bedroom in my apartment.

The arm around my waist tightens and memories of last night flood my body. Waking up to Jaxon toying with my breast. Begging Jaxon to have sex with me. Feeling Jaxon bury himself deep inside me.

It was incredible. What I wouldn't give to spend every night the way we did last night. Jaxon laughing and joking with me. Totally relaxed and unguarded.

Except we agreed it would be a one time thing. My stomach dips. I don't want last night to be the last time Jaxon touches me. I want him to touch me every chance he gets. I want him to choose me.

Shit. I'm catching feelings for my fake husband.

The same man who ghosted me after we kissed. How the hell is he going to react after we had sex together? Is he going to run for the hills?

I can't handle it. His rejection after the kiss was hard enough. His rejection after sex would leave a permanent scar.

I need to get out of here. Escape before Jaxon gets the chance to give me the brush off.

But how?

I lift his arm. He grunts and presses his hard length against my ass. I inch toward the edge of the bed. He sighs before rolling over. Phew.

I slide out of bed and hurry to my suitcase. I grab my clothes for the day before rushing to the bathroom. I don't shower. The sound of water would wake Jaxon. No thanks. Instead, I quickly wash and dress.

When I finish, I slowly open the door and peek out. Jaxon is sleeping while facing away from me. This is my chance. I run to the door and hurry outside.

Only once I'm walking the path toward the main building do I realize I don't have my phone or my purse. Shit. I stop and nibble on my lip as I contemplate what to do.

"I didn't expect you to come," Stacey says and I startle. Where did she appear from?

"Sorry?"

"I figured you'd skip the spa day since you didn't show up for the lunch or wine tasting yesterday."

The spa day? What is she... Oh, right. The wedding. The reason we're here. The reason Jaxon is pretending to be my husband.

Except he is my husband. In name only.

My sore inner muscles remind me our marriage wasn't in name only last night.

I force all my crazy thoughts away. "A spa day sounds wonderful."

She rakes her gaze over me. "You appear to need it."

I fist my hand before I reach for my hair. I didn't have time to straighten it this morning. My curls are probably bursting out of my bun.

"You know how it is." I smirk. "Being a newlywed and not getting any sleep."

Her eyes narrow on me. "Newlywed. Right."

I wave my wedding ring at her. "Newly married."

She starts to speak but I hurl questions at her before she has a chance to spout another nasty remark.

"Did you pick out your wedding rings together? Or is it a surprise? Alan does love giving surprises."

Crappy surprises delivered by a process server. The asshole.

The door behind Stacey opens up and a woman I recognize from the rehearsal dinner as one of Stacey's bridesmaids pops her head out. "They're ready for us."

Stacey whirls around and stomps to the door. I debate escaping but the temptation of annoying Alan's fiancée all morning is too much for me to resist. I follow her into the spa, where three other women are waiting for us.

"Who's this?" one of them asks.

"This is Alan's ex-wife," Stacey says. Damn. I thought she believed our charade.

"I'm not Alan's ex-wife. We were never married."

"Really?" Stacey crosses her arms over her chest and glares at me. "You didn't own a house together?"

"You don't have to be married to own a house together."

"You acted as husband and wife."

Someone obviously thinks she can somehow get me to trip up, and therefore, Alan will win the lawsuit. Not on my watch.

"Nope. Alan was never my husband. He never proposed. He never gave me a ring. We never said our vows. Unlike Jaxon." I sigh as I study my ring. "He whisked me away for our wedding."

"Sounds romantic," one of the bridesmaids says.

"Oh, sorry." I pretend to startle. "I don't believe we've met. I'm Blossom."

"I'm Jenny. And this is Amy and Tiffany."

"We're the bridesmaids," Amy says.

I scan the room. "I thought there were five of you."

Tiffany giggles. "Emily and Paula are indisposed."

"Indisposed how?"

Jenny rolls her eyes. "Emily can't handle her tequila, and Paula picked up one of the groomsmen."

"Which one?" I ask as I sit next to her. "Do you have a picture?"

She digs her phone out of her purse and flips through the pictures until she finds the image. "I don't remember his name."

Unfortunately, I recognize him. "It's Glen. He's one of Alan's best friends."

Tiffany peers over Jenny's shoulders. "He's cute."

"He's a player." Glen always gave me the creeps. He was not discriminate about where he'd stick his dick. In fact, he hit on me more than once. Pretty much every time he got drunk, he'd corner me and try to get me to give him a 'taste'.

"Glen isn't a player anymore," Stacey says.

"He picked up Paula." Picking up a bridesmaid the night before the wedding is the definition of player.

"They've been circling around each other for months now."

Awesome. Stacey has decided to be contrary all day. This spa experience is going to be so very relaxing. Maybe I should leave. But guessing by the gleam in Stacey's eyes, she's goading me to bail. I'm not letting her win.

A woman enters the reception area. "Good morning," she greets. "I'm Maeve. If you'd follow me, we have you all set up for mani/pedis."

"I thought we were doing facials and massages," Stacey says.

"Don't worry. We have you all set up for facials and massages after your mani/pedis."

"Good," Stacey mutters as she flounces through the door Maeve is holding open. Jenny and Amy follow her.

"Stacey is a perfectionist," Tiffany explains as we trail behind the other bridesmaids.

Stacey, Jenny, and Amy are already seated when we reach the spa area. I maneuver Tiffany into the chair next to Stacey before sitting on the end away from the rest of them.

"Champagne?" Maeve arrives with a tray of champagne glasses.

"To our girl getting married!" Amy shouts as she lifts her glass in the air.

"Finally," Tiffany mutters next to me and I nearly choke on my champagne. Maybe today won't be as bad as I'd feared.

"What is this?" Stacey mutters before shouting, "Maeve! I need another glass. This champagne is not drinkable."

Tiffany sighs. "And so it begins."

"What begins?" I whisper.

"Stacey's perfectionism can switch to bitchiness at the turn of a hat."

I can't argue with her since Stacey is currently berating Maeve for the quality of the champagne.

"Why are you friends with her?"

Tiffany shrugs. "We've known each other since high school."

"I can bring you a different bottle, but it'll be an additional cost," Maeve says to Stacey.

"Not a problem. We'll have plenty of money soon enough." Stacey narrows her eyes on me in challenge.

I do love a challenge.

I widen my eyes and pretend I have no idea she's referring to Alan winning the lawsuit against me. "Is Alan getting a raise?"

"You know exactly why we'll have plenty of money soon."

"You're getting a raise? Congrats. I didn't catch what you do for work."

"At least I don't make beer."

"Too bad for you. Brewing beer is fun and exciting and challenging. I love my job."

Stacey snorts. "Of course, you do. You have no class."

I bark out a laugh. "You are hilarious. I have no class, but it doesn't stop you from trying to steal my money. Precious."

Her hand fists on her glass until her knuckles are white. "It's not your money. Half of it is Alan's."

"He doesn't deserve half of my inheritance because he was my boyfriend when my parents died."

"Then, why is he winning the lawsuit?"

"Winning the lawsuit?" I chuckle. "Did he tell you he's winning? He's lying. I'm not surprised. He is a liar and a cheater after all."

"He only cheated on you because you were horrible in bed. A dead fish is how he referred to you."

"Wow. Victim shaming. Very high class."

"Get out!" She flings her hand toward the door and her champagne flies all over her. "Look what you made me do."

I down the rest of my champagne before standing. "Have a lovely day. I can't wait for this afternoon when you marry a man who will never be faithful to you."

I saunter off. A glass breaks on the wall behind me but I ignore it. I'm done lowering myself to Stacey's level.

Chapter 21

"Go ahead. Underestimate me." ~ Jaxon

JAXON

Even before I open my eyes, I can sense Blossom is gone. I don't know how to feel about her leaving. I'm relieved I don't have to speak with her since I have no idea how to react after last night.

But I'm also angry she left without a word. Did she not feel our connection last night? Maybe it's better if she didn't, since we would never work together anyway.

I roll out of bed to search the chalet. I find Blossom's purse and her phone, but there's no sign of the woman herself.

Maybe she only stepped out for a minute. The cold sheet in the bed says otherwise.

Do I go look for her? Do I confront her about last night?

I don't know how to react to this situation.

I do the same thing I always do when faced with a situation I don't know how to deal with. I don my swimming trunks and make my way to the ocean. I don't have my scull here for my usual morning rowing session, so I'll have to settle for a swim.

When I reach the beach and spot the group huddled in a circle on the sand, I nearly turn around. Unfortunately, Miles notices me before I have the chance.

"There's the groom now!" he shouts as he waves.

I swallow my groan and join my brothers. "What are you doing here? Isn't this a private beach?"

Zane snorts. "A beach can't be owned."

Technically, it can, but my free-spirited brother thinks otherwise. I don't waste my time arguing with him.

Kai throws an arm around my shoulders. "We're here to support you. How did it feel to lose your virginity at twenty-eight?"

I elbow him and he flies away while cackling with laughter. "I wasn't a virgin."

"There's no reason to be ashamed of waiting until you were married," Miles says.

"How long have they been making virgin jokes?" I ask Eli.

"All morning."

"Is this why all of you are here? To make fun of my wedding night?"

"Wedding night? Sure, it was." Zane winks.

"I don't know." Kai points to my back. "He has fingernail marks on his shoulders."

"I'm confused," Miles says as he confirms the marks. "I thought the wedding was fake."

"Their kiss didn't seem fake." Kai smacks his lips together.

Zane pushes him. "Don't you know how to do a fake kiss?"

Kai shoves Zane, who stumbles into Miles. The three end up tumbling to the ground. Nothing new there.

I address Eli. "You swore by barnacle, booze, and brotherhood, not to tell them."

He shrugs. "Except for the lawsuit, they figured it out for themselves."

"How?"

Rhett slaps me on the back. "You made us put together a wedding in an hour. It wasn't difficult to figure out."

I scowl at him. "Are you saying I'm not spontaneous?"

He laughs. "I'm saying you've never taken action without spending months planning and studying how to proceed."

I snap my mouth shut. I have no response since he's right.

"But you did for Blossom. You must really like her."

I do. Blossom is unlike any woman I've ever met before. She's smart and competitive. Has the most gorgeous brown eyes that change colors based on her moods. Is absolutely beautiful. And is sexy as hell. Sinking deep inside her last night felt better than heaven.

But she also talks all the time, thrives in group settings, and enjoys socializing. She'd be bored of my simple life in no time. And she's a mainlander. They never last long on the island.

"It doesn't matter."

Rhett frowns. "Why not?"

"Blossom would never stay with me."

"Why not?" Eli asks.

I roll my eyes. "Don't be obtuse."

"Who's being obtuse?" Miles asks as he returns to us covered in sand. Zane and Kai trail after him.

Eli points to me. "Jaxon is."

Zane's eyes widen. "Jaxon obtuse? He's the smartest one of all the Raider brothers."

Kai elbows him. "It's obviously an emotional jab."

"Oh." Zane nods. "Understandable."

I glare at my younger brothers. "I'm not emotionally stunted."

"You tend not to notice the obvious when it comes to emotions," Zane says.

"Such as a woman who wants you throwing yourself at her," Kai adds.

I noticed Blossom. How could I not? She's beautiful, and when she enters a room, you can't miss it since she brings sunshine with her.

"Blossom is not the woman for me."

Eli crosses his arms over his chest. "Except you married her."

"To stop Alan from stealing from her."

"Alan's an asshole. Can we prank him?" Kai asks.

"Or beat the shit out of him?" Miles adds.

"Whoa!" I hold up my hands. "Nobody's beating the shit out of anybody. It won't help the lawsuit. Speaking of lawsuit." I glare at my brothers. "If you tell anyone about it, I will unleash pranking skills the likes you have never seen before on you."

Kai frowns. "But I'm the prank champion."

"And I have a degree in chemistry."

Eli shivers. "You don't want a person who has a degree in chemistry coming after you. Trust me. I know."

Rhett bumps his shoulder. "You love it when Paisley pranks you."

Eli grins. "I can get really inventive with my punishments."

My stomach sours. I want what he has. A woman who loves me. A woman who will stick by my side no matter what. But Blossom isn't that woman. We're too different. I can't take a chance on a woman who will end up leaving me the second she gets bored.

"If you're done invading my personal life, I'm going for a swim." I don't wait for a response, I march toward the water.

I don't make it far. Rhett steps in front of me and the rest of my interfering brothers surround me.

"Are you going to give this relationship with Blossom a chance?" Rhett asks.

I frown. "I married Blossom to force her ex to drop the lawsuit. This isn't a relationship. It's an arrangement."

"It wasn't an arrangement last night." Eli nods to the marks on my shoulders.

"We agreed it would be a one time thing."

"Let's vote," Miles says. "Who votes for Jaxon to give Blossom a chance?"

I roll my eyes when all of my brothers raise their hands.

"Too bad you don't get a vote in my relationship status." I try to push past Rhett but he doesn't budge. "What now?"

"I want you to be happy."

"I am happy. I have a job I love and a family who drives me crazy."

Eli squeezes my shoulder. "What about a woman you love?"

My heart skips a beat. I don't love Blossom. Loving her would be a sure way to get my heart broken when she decides to move on.

"I told you. Blossom isn't the woman for me."

"Oh god. He's going to dump Blossom and go back to dating Melanie types again." Miles groans. "They're so boring."

"We prefer Blossom to Melanies," Kai says.

"What part of you don't get a vote, do you not understand?" I ask.

"The part where we're forced to pretend to like Melanies at family meals," Zane says.

I huff. "There was only one Melanie."

"Was there?" Zane asks. "All of the women you date are the same."

"Bor-ing!" Kai and Miles shout in unison before high-fiving each other.

"Blossom's not boring," Eli says.

I narrow my eyes on him. "You're supposed to be the voice of reason when these three hooligans get out of control."

"I am being the voice of reason. Blossom isn't boring, and you like her. Why don't you give this relationship a chance?"

I cross my arms over my chest. "Are you saying all my previous girlfriends were boring?"

"We're not discussing Melanie. We're discussing Blossom."

"I'm not discussing Blossom. I'm going for a swim."

I try to walk around Eli but he shackles my wrist to stop me. I slam my hand down on his inner elbow and he immediately releases me with a grunt.

"Fuck. I forgot what a dirty fighter you are."

Naturally, I'm a dirty fighter. I have five brothers – three of whom think fighting is fun.

"I'm done discussing this. Unless anyone else wants to fight me."

I glare at my brothers until they drop their gazes.

"Good," I mutter as I make my way to the water's edge.

I kick off my shoes and dive into the ocean.

As I swim, thoughts invade. What if they're right? Maybe I should give Blossom a chance. Maybe our differences don't matter. Maybe she'll stay on the island.

I snort and nearly inhale a bucketful of salt water.

Enough of this contemplation. I know the truth. Blossom isn't the woman I'm searching for.

I speed up my strokes and kick my feet faster until I can't think anymore. Until the only thing I can concentrate on is the water and the next stroke.

Chapter 22

"Apparently, a wedding doesn't have to be romantic."
~ Blossom

BLOSSOM

I'm laying on the bed in the chalet, dozing, when Jaxon returns. I sit up. "Where have you been?"

"I could ask you the same thing."

"I went to the bridal spa day." I was also escaping from the awkward morning after talk but I avoid mentioning how much of a coward I was. I promise I'm not usually a scaredy-cat, afraid to discuss my emotions. I also don't usually marry a man who ghosted me for months either. "Or, at least, I tried to."

He frowns. "What happened?"

"In a word. Stacey is a bitch and she deserves Alan."

"You sound surprised."

"Nope. I'm not." I notice he's wearing wet swimming trunks. "Did you go swimming?"

"I usually row every morning for an hour, but I had to settle for swimming this morning."

"Rowing every morning sounds awesome. Witnessing the sun rise over the ocean." I sigh. "Smuggler's Hideaway is such a magical place."

His brow wrinkles. "You really think the island is magical?"

"What do you mean? You've lived here all your life. You must realize how charming this place is."

"Charming? There's a seal who thinks it's a road stop."

I gasp. "Don't you dare make fun of Sammy the seal."

"And there are a ton of holiday celebrations with unique and often strange customs," he continues.

"You better not be dissing *The Smuggler's Gauntlet.* It was awesome." I grin. "And we won."

"And let's not forget *Mermaid Karaoke.*"

I wave a hand in dismissal. "*Mermaid Karaoke* doesn't bother me. Let them have fun, I say. They're not harming anyone."

His brow furrows. "You really like the island?"

"Um, yeah. I chose to live here."

He checks the time. "You better start getting ready. The wedding's in two hours."

I groan. "I've peopled enough today. Can we skip the wedding?"

He frowns at me. "Peopled enough today? But you love people."

"There's a limit to how much I enjoy people."

"Do you want to skip the wedding because you still have feelings for Alan?"

"I'm sorry." I pretend to clean my ears. "I must be going deaf because you did not just accuse me of still having feelings for Alan."

"I wouldn't use the term accuse."

I jump off the bed and stomp over to him. "I do not have feelings for that man." I poke his chest. "Do. You. Understand?"

He captures my hand and lays it against his chest. His shirt is soaked, allowing me to feel his defined muscles. And now I want to skip the wedding for an entirely different reason. A dirty, sweaty, get naked reason.

"You don't want to avoid the wedding because of him?"

I roll my eyes. "Are you serious? I could have said no to his wedding invitation. But I didn't. I don't run away from my problems."

"But you don't want to attend the wedding. I'm confused."

My brow wrinkles. "You're an introvert. How can you be confused about me not wanting to people anymore today?"

"You're not an introvert."

"Doesn't mean I always want to spend time with people."

He studies me for a few seconds before nodding. "Okay. We'll say I got sunburned and am too unwell to attend."

I rake my gaze over his tanned figure. "Except Alan has met you and knows you're already tan."

"Let me think." He taps his foot as he tries to come up with another excuse.

"It's okay. We came here for the wedding. We're going to the wedding. I was just being a whiner."

"You are not a whiner."

I giggle. "I've got you fooled."

He frowns and I push up on my toes to kiss his cheek. "I was joking."

His scent hits me and I lean closer. Bad, Blossom. Bad. This is a fake marriage. Time to get your butt moving toward the real marriage of the weekend.

"I need to shower," I mumble before rushing off to gather my things.

"I'll be on the back deck."

"I'm not kicking you out."

He nods toward the glass panel between the shower and the chalet. The see-through glass panel. "Oh."

"Yeah. Oh."

I watch as he shuts the sliding glass door behind him. Does he not want to watch me shower? Should I have made it clear he's welcome to watch me? My body tingles at the thought of soaping up my breasts while Jaxon watches through the window.

"Fake, Blossom. Fake." Maybe if I remind myself out loud, it'll help.

Ninety minutes later, we're walking toward the wedding venue.

"I'm glad the ceremony is inside."

"I thought you enjoyed weddings on the beach."

"Alan knows I want a beach wedding."

"Ah. And you didn't want him to steal the idea."

I nod. "It sounds petty but I'm allowed to be a little petty today."

He squeezes my elbow. "You're not being petty. Watching your ex marry someone else in your dream wedding ceremony is not a trivial matter."

"For a socially awkward whiskey distiller, you know the right thing to say at the right time."

His cheeks warm and he slides his glasses up his nose. "Thank you?"

We reach the event room where the ceremony is happening and find seats in the back, away from everyone else. I notice several people crane their necks to get a glimpse of us. I smile and wave at all of them.

That's right, folks. I leveled up.

Jaxon squirms in his seat next to me. "Do you know seventeen tons of gold are made into wedding rings each year in the United States?"

"Really? I thought gold wasn't used as much since white gold and platinum have gained in popularity."

"White gold is an alloy containing about 75% gold and about 25% nickel and zinc. It was originally developed to imitate platinum."

"Oh, right. Meaning three-quarters of white gold wedding rings count as gold."

"And gold is usually cheaper than platinum," he adds.

"I'm aware. Only about 150 tons of platinum are mined a year."

Jaxon's eyes widen in surprise and I slap his shoulder.

"Did you forget I have a degree in chemical engineering?"

He clears his throat. "I've never met anyone who had a degree in chemical engineering but wasn't..." He trails off. "Never mind."

I know exactly what he's thinking, but I can't help wanting to tease him. "Wasn't what?"

He fiddles with his glasses as he contemplates the floor of the room. "Um..."

He's adorable when he's flustered. I need to fluster him more often. Except he's going to ghost me as soon as this wedding weekend is over. I scowl.

"I'm sorry." He squeezes my hand. "I didn't mean to call you a nerd."

I don't care if he calls me a nerd, but I roll with his apology. It's better than thinking about how this man has been the sweetest, kindest man to me this weekend but it's all a charade.

"How could you think I'm a nerd?" I challenge.

"Um..."

I bark out a laugh. "I got you."

"You were making fun of me?" he grumbles.

"Not making fun of you. I love how comfortable you are in your skin. It's a great trait."

"But you laughed at me."

"I didn't laugh at you. I laughed at how I misled you. At how clever I am."

His brow wrinkles. "You laughed at how clever you are?"

I open my mouth to respond but the person in front of me clears her throat. I frown at her. "What?"

She nods to the front of the room where Alan is standing with his groomsmen. He's also glaring at us. Geez. Am I not allowed to have fun at his wedding? He's the one who invited me.

I wave. His eyes narrow and he steps forward but the music begins and his best man pulls him back to his spot.

"You may not care for Alan," Jaxon whispers to me, "but he still cares for you."

"He doesn't care about me. He wants my money. And for me to be miserable without him."

The first bridesmaid glides down the aisle. I have to bite my lip when I see what she's wearing.

The dress looks like a fight broke out between a corset and a cocktail napkin and bad taste won. The top is strapless with a sweetheart neckline, leaving little to the imagination. Especially when you add the sheer mesh panels with enough visible boning to warrant a PG-13 warning.

And the skirt? Flouncy, flirty, and dangerously short. One wrong breeze and the bridesmaids will be flashing half the wedding guests.

"If this is the *bridesmaid* dress, I'm scared to ask what the bride's wearing."

"Lingerie and a tiara?" Jaxon suggests and I have to slap a hand over my mouth before I bark out another laugh and earn the wrath of Alan once again.

"You're trouble," I mutter to him.

"There's more to me than meets the eye."

I am well aware. I have not only glimpsed beneath those nerdy clothes. I thought I reached the holy land when I did because holy mermaids swimming the sea! Someone's been working out.

I've been inexplicably drawn to Jaxon since we first met. And since I've been getting to know him? I'm even more drawn to him.

I need to reinforce those steel walls around my heart before this weekend ends with me having a broken heart.

Chapter 23

"Someone should write a book with all the questions that are considered rude to ask." ~ Jaxon

JAXON

"I thought I'd seen it all growing up on Smuggler's Hideaway," I say as I escort Blossom from the ceremony toward where the drinks and dinner are happening.

"Jenny was right. Emily can't handle her tequila." Blossom giggles. "I thought Stacey was going to lose her mind when her bridesmaid threw up in the potted plant. But I didn't expect her to start screaming at Emily."

"Or for her to slap Alan when he interfered to calm her down." The slap was loud. It sounded painful.

"You should never tell a woman in a full-blown hissy fit to calm down."

"Duly noted."

"Still, she shouldn't have slapped him. I thought their marriage was over before it began."

"My brothers would have already started a betting sheet on how long the marriage lasts." Normally, I find my brothers a bit overly anxious to start bets, but in this case, I wouldn't blame them.

"I give them three months." Blossom leans close to whisper, "Less if the lawsuit gets dismissed sooner."

"Do you think Stacey is with him for his money?" I ask as we enter the room where the reception is being held.

She sweeps her arm over the room. "This can't have been cheap."

She's right. I'm not interested in material things but even I can recognize how expensive the centerpieces, aisle florals, tablecloths, and plates are. Not to mention how there are two wedding planners running around. How much money is Blossom's inheritance anyway?

"Why do you suddenly appear constipated?" Blossom's nose wrinkles. "Do you need to use the restroom? We passed one on our way here."

"I'm not constipated."

She circles my face. "This is the appearance of a constipated man."

I blow out a breath. "I'm not constipated. I have a question for you, but I think it's inappropriate to ask."

"If it's whether I'm wearing panties, the answer is yes. I'm wearing a thong."

I groan. I was having a hard enough time keeping my cock under control with the dress she's wearing. It hugs her curves in all the right places. Curves I've touched with my hands and mouth. Curves, I'm anxious to touch again.

And now I know she's wearing a thong. A thong that leaves her ass cheeks free. Blossom has a magnificent ass. I want to watch it bounce while I plunge into her from behind.

"You're cruel."

She bats her eyelashes. "Me? I'm only trying to help you out since you're afraid to ask your question." She taps her chin. "Is it whether I'm wearing a bra? I'm not."

My cock springs to life. It hardens and lengthens before pressing against my zipper, intent on getting to Blossom.

I step closer to her until we're chest to chest. Her breath hitches, and her breasts rub against my chest. Breasts I now know aren't constrained in a bra.

"You're lucky we're in public," I growl.

She widens her eyes and feigns innocence. "Yeah? Why?"

"Because otherwise I'd bend you over the nearest table and fuck you from behind."

Her brown eyes darken to burnt umber as a blush spreads from her cheeks down her neck to the top of her dress. My cock hardens until it's harder than steel.

"Who's stopping you?"

"I'm not an exhibitionist."

Her shoulders drop. "Darn."

"You're trouble." I palm her neck and squeeze.

She winks. "But I'm fun."

Yes, she is. I've never had this much fun with a partner before. Usually, my romantic partners are perfectly pleasant, but they don't laugh and joke. Interesting. Maybe my brothers are right. Maybe my partners have all been boring until Blossom.

You can say many things about Blossom, but she isn't boring. And she's definitely fun.

"What's your question, Jaxon? Ask away."

"It may be construed as rude." I'm not always the best in judging what's considered rude by society. "I don't want to offend you."

"You won't offend me, but I may not answer."

I meet her gaze. She doesn't avoid my eyes. She looks straight at me. Okay, she's not lying.

"How much is your inheritance?"

"You only thought to ask this question now?"

I shrug. "It's not my business, but..."

"But?" She prods.

"Alan and Stacey have spent a lot of money on this wedding, considering he's a tire salesman."

"I thought Stacey had money but she made it clear during our 'spa' morning that they're expecting a large sum of money soon. Spoiler alert. The large sum of money is their share of my inheritance when they win the lawsuit."

I growl. "They're not winning the lawsuit."

She pets my chest as if to comfort me. She shouldn't be comforting me. I should be the one doing the comforting. She's the one dealing with an ex trying to steal from her. And here I am asking questions that are none of my business.

"Eight hundred thousand dollars." When I don't immediately respond, she prattles on. "I know. No one thinks I come from money. Hell, I didn't realize my parents had saved up so much. But..."

I place a finger on her lips to stop her. "My silence has nothing to do with thinking you don't come from money or don't have class or whatever bullshit you're telling yourself. I'm fighting the urge to find Alan and beat the shit out of him."

She blinks up at me. "Beat the shit out of him?"

"I could do it. I have five brothers. I've been fighting since the first time Miles threw his dirty diaper at me."

"I believe you. I've seen how strong your upper body is." She blushes. "I was surprised you want to beat him up."

"He's trying to steal nearly half a million dollars from you."

"I know. I read the complaint."

"I thought this was an argument over ten thousand dollars. I didn't realize it was an argument about a fortune."

"I don't care how much the money is. I care how my ex-boyfriend, who cheated on me multiple times and planned to spend my money without consulting me, thinks he has a right to the money my parents left me. Money, I only have because they died when I was twenty-six. My mom will never shop for a wedding dress with me. My dad will never walk me down the aisle."

My heart squeezes at the pain in her voice. "I'm sorry I didn't give you the wedding you deserve."

She closes her eyes and inhales a deep breath. When she opens her eyes again, they're no longer shiny. "You gave me exactly what I needed. Thank you."

"You never have to thank me," I grumble.

"But I want to."

"Excuse me." Someone bumps into me from behind and I remember we're standing in a very public place, having an extremely private conversation.

I offer Blossom my arm. "Shall we?"

She threads her arm through mine. "Let's find our table."

We meander through the room past tables until we find ours. There are already two couples seated at the round table when we arrive.

"I'm Jaxon and this is Blossom," I introduce as I pull out Blossom's chair for her.

"I'm Hugo and this is my wife, Lilian," the man on my left introduces.

"And I'm Crispin and this is Diana," the man next to Blossom says.

Silence falls on the table. I scramble to think of polite conversation. I usually avoid small talk, but this is one of those situations where I believe Eli would tell me it's required.

"And what do you do for work, Crispin? Diana?" Blossom asks and I blow out a breath in relief. Naturally, she knows how to handle the situation. I'm coming to find she can handle most any situation.

"I'm an investment banker," Crispin answers.

"How did you meet Alan?"

Crispin sips on his water before answering. "Alan is preparing for when he receives a large inheritance. He asked me for advice."

Blossom's hands fist in her lap. I capture one and slowly peel her fingers apart before placing it on my thigh.

She gives Crispin her back. "And how do you know Alan, Hugo?"

"I'm his car dealer. And what do you do, Jaxon?"

I don't enjoy the attention on me, but I'll do anything to keep the subject away from Alan's 'inheritance'.

"I'm the lead distiller at *Buccaneer's Whiskey & Distillery.*"

Crispin's nose wrinkles. "You make whiskey? Do you work with your hands?"

"I find it fascinating," Blossom says before I have the chance to answer. "I brew beer, which I love. But whiskey distilling is a more delicate art."

Crispin appears appalled. "You brew beer?"

"Yep. I'm the assistant to the brewmaster at *Five Fathoms Brewing.* It's a local brewery here on the island."

Diana leans forward. "You seriously brew beer? And he distills whiskey?"

"Actually, Jaxon is being shy. He's also part-owner of the distillery."

Crispin's eyes spark. "Part-owner. Let me give you my card." He pats his chest, but before he can pull out a card, Blossom stops him.

"Thank you, but no thank you. We already have an investment banker on the island."

He sputters but the servers arrive with our wine. Once he's distracted, I lean close to whisper in Blossom's ear. "You don't have to protect me. I can handle questions from strangers."

She shrugs. "It's no trouble. You don't enjoy small talk. I don't mind. I'll be your buffer."

I quite enjoy having a buffer. A sexy buffer, I want to spend all night buried inside.

There's more to Blossom than I originally thought. Yes, she's different than me. But we have things in common as well. Maybe she's not my complete opposite after all. And she does love Smuggler's Hideaway. Maybe we could have a future together.

Chapter 24

"Now that was unexpected." ~ Blossom

BLOSSOM

I spend the rest of dinner batting questions away from Jaxon. I had to open my big mouth and tell the people at the table he's part owner of the distillery? I shouldn't have, but they were looking down their noses at us and I couldn't stand it.

Especially after Crispin said Alan expects to come into money. Come into money? Is that what we're calling stealing these days?

Jaxon brushes the hair off my neck. "How are you doing?"

"Wondering how much jail time I'd get for beating up a wedding guest."

He chuckles. "The jail cells in Smuggler's Rest are quite nice."

"How would you know?"

"Have you not met my brothers?"

I giggle. "You have a point."

"I think Eli's debating between donating money for a new jailhouse or hiring a matchmaker for my brothers."

"I pity the women who fall in love with Kai, Zane, or Miles. They are not going to be easy to pin down."

"I think Kai has already found a woman."

"Really? I haven't heard he's dating anyone." And, trust me, I would have heard. Gossiping is an island sport. A competitive sport.

"They're not dating. She won't give him the time of day."

My jaw drops. "No way. A Raider brother was shot down?"

"As I recall, your best friend, Dakota, shot Rhett down plenty."

I sniff. "He deserved it."

He drops a kiss on my nose. "I believe you."

He needs to stop with the little kisses and touches and caresses. If I didn't know better, I'd think our relationship was real. But I do know better. Our relationship is fake. No matter how comfortable the diamond ring feels on my finger. We are not real.

"Do you want to hang around longer? Do some dancing?"

I raise an eyebrow. "I think you'll break my toes with these shoes."

I kick out my foot to show off my high-heeled sandal.

"I wouldn't want to break your toe." His voice is gruff and when I meet his gaze, his eyes are flaring with passion. Passion? I decide to test the theory and cross my legs. He groans before adjusting himself.

"No dancing then. Do you want to stay for the cutting of the cake and all the other silly wedding traditions?"

"Silly traditions? You don't enjoy weddings?"

My nose wrinkles. "I enjoy them just fine when I don't know the bride and groom aren't spending money they expect to steal from me."

He stands and offers me his hand. "Let's go then. You can soak in the hot tub on the deck while the sun sets with a glass of wine."

"Can we steal a bottle of wine from here?" I ask as he pulls me to my feet. My feet protest but I ignore the pain. I am not complaining about walking in heels when Jaxon thinks they're sexy.

He chuckles. "I should have known."

"It's not actually stealing since we're guests," I claim.

He leads me to the bar with a hand on my lower back. I shiver at the feel of those big, capable hands touching my body. The material of my dress is thin, but not thin enough. I want his hands on my naked body.

"Do you want a bottle of red or white?"

"Duh. A bottle of bubbly."

"Why did I ask?" he mutters.

We're nearly at the bar when Alan steps in our way.

I force a smile. "Congratulations, Alan. I hope you'll be happy for many years."

"I won't allow you to disparage my wife."

"Your wife? I thought I was your wife."

Jaxon growls. "You're my wife."

Alan's nostrils flare as he faces off with me. "You know who I mean. I won't allow you to treat Stacey this way."

"What way? What are you talking about?"

I have a sneaking suspicion the bride has been lying about me. Big surprise there. I had her pegged as a saint who never lies. Not. I bite my tongue before I laugh in Alan's face. I don't want to escalate the situation.

Alan grinds his teeth and his ears turn red. "Don't act all innocent. You know what you did."

"Um, no. I don't." This is technically not a lie. Since I didn't disparage Stacey.

He steps closer but Jaxon pushes me behind him. "Stop. You don't intimidate *my wife*. You don't get up all in her space and spin lies about her."

My body gets all tingly at Jaxon's words. A man hasn't defended me since my dad died over two years ago. If you had asked me this morning what I think about a man defending me, I would have told you I can defend myself.

But now? My nipples are pebbled, and my panties are damp. I haven't been this turned on while dressed in forever. As in it's never happened before. Oh my. Jaxon is one sexy beast.

Alan stabs Jaxon in the chest with his finger. "What about how your wife treated my wife this morning? Stacey came back to our hotel room in tears."

"If Stacey was in tears, I had nothing to do with it."

Alan tries to push past Jaxon to get to me, but Jaxon maneuvers him away.

"You lied to her," Alan says. "You told her to enjoy her marriage with a man who won't be faithful to her."

"I'm not hearing the lie in this statement."

"I have never cheated on Stacey."

I peek around Jaxon and lift a brow at Alan. "Really? This is me. The woman with photographic proof of your inability to keep your tiny dick in your pants."

"I only cheated on you because you were a horrible lay. A dead fish would be better at sex than you."

Jaxon growls before he steps forward. "Do not speak about my wife and sex again or you'll regret it."

"Oh yeah? What are you going to do, nerd? Hit me with a physics book?" Alan pretends to search for a book on Jaxon. "Your hands are empty. No nerdy books to be found."

"I'm warning you one more time to shut the hell up before you regret it."

Alan snorts. "I'm not afraid of you."

Jaxon smirks. "You should be."

And then – bam! – Jaxon punches Alan in the nose. Blood spurts everywhere as Alan screams in pain. It's possible I'm cheering but only on the inside. If I had pompoms, it would be different.

"You asshole! You broke my nose!"

"I warned you." Jaxon fiddles with his cufflinks as Alan yells for help.

"Police! Police!"

I tug on Jaxon's hand. "We should go. I don't want you to get arrested."

"Don't worry. I know all of the police officers on the island. They'll never arrest me."

"You're crazy. Certifiable. How did I not know this about you?"

Hudson rushes into the room, followed by a bunch of security.

Alan points to Jaxon. "I want him arrested. He punched me without reason."

Jaxon glares at him. "There was a reason. Do I need to remind you?"

"He's threatening me! You heard him!"

"I'll handle this," Hudson says as he motions for Jaxon to proceed him out of the room. I rush to follow them.

We arrive in an office and Hudson shuts the door behind us. "We'll sit this out in here until Alan is calmed down. But I advise you not to return to the party."

"We are not going back to the wedding. The groom is an asshole." Jaxon rubs his hand.

"Shit. Are you hurt?" I pull his hand to me to examine it. "Your knuckles are bruised. We should get you some ice."

"Alan has a hard head."

I snort. "You're telling me. I don't think he listened to my advice once when we were together."

Hudson's brow wrinkles. "Why did you go to the wedding of your ex if you don't like him?"

I wrinkle my nose. "It's a long story."

"I'll probably hear it from my wife, Nova."

"No, you won't," Jaxon grumbles. "No one is going to spread Blossom's private business around the island."

I bump his hip. "You better stop being nice to me or I'll think you like me."

Hudson's gaze ping pongs between us. "Aren't you two married?"

"It's a—"

"… long story," he finishes for me.

There's a knock on the door. "Hudson. We could use your help out here."

Hudson sighs. "I hate wedding season," he mutters before opening the door.

A man hands him an ice pack. "This is for Rocky Balboa."

Jaxon accepts the ice with a purse of his lips. "Rocky lost. I did not."

"The groom is throwing a fit. I think speaking to *the* Hudson Clark would go a long way in helping to calm him down."

"I'll go," Hudson steps into the hallway. "You can sneak out the back hallway."

"But I didn't get to steal a bottle of wine," I complain.

He chuckles. "I'll have a bottle of champagne sent to your chalet if you promise to behave."

I raise my hands. "I'm not the one with the fisticuffs."

Jaxon grunts. "As long as Alan doesn't spread any more lies about Blossom, I'm good."

Hudson's eyes narrow. "He's spreading lies about a local? I guess he's getting his wish to meet me now."

I hurry to the door and watch Hudson prowl down the hallway. His anger is evident in every step he makes.

"Thanks for calling me a local," I shout after him.

He flicks his hand in what I assume is a gesture of 'you're welcome'.

"You ready to get out of here?" I ask Jaxon.

He offers me his hand, but instead of leading me out of the room, he hauls me near. "Are you okay?"

"Why wouldn't I be okay? I didn't punch anyone or break my nose."

He leans his forehead against mine. "Alan said some nasty things about you. Words can hurt."

My heart pounds in my chest. This man is everything. His knuckles are bruised and yet he's worried about me. And why are his knuckles bruised? Because he was defending me.

There's no denying it. I have utterly failed to keep my heart encased in steel. I'm falling for Jaxon.

I cuddle into Jaxon's warmth. "Yeah, words can hurt. But when a man defends you by breaking the speaker's nose it's all good."

"You're good?" I nod. He squeezes me once before motioning to the door. "Then, let's get out of here."

He wraps an arm around my shoulders and we make our way to the chalet. All the while my heart is beating out of control.

I'm falling for Jaxon. And we only have one more night together.

Chapter 25

JAXON

I pace the chalet as I attempt to calm down. Between being hard all night for Blossom and fighting with her asshole ex, my blood is pumping and my adrenaline is flowing.

Blossom exits the bathroom wearing that sleepshirt I can see through and I fist my hands to stop myself from going to her and pulling her into my arms before stripping her bare and having my way with her.

"I thought you wanted to go in the hot tub."

She gestures outside. "It's raining."

Crap. I'm too distracted. I hadn't even noticed it started raining.

There's a knock on the door and she spins around to answer it. I growl. She's not answering the door in her sleepshirt. No man gets to see her this way. Only me.

"I've got it," I say as I push her behind me.

She rolls her eyes. "Whatever, caveman."

I answer the door and a man grins at me. "I have your champagne and strawberries and chocolate."

He starts to roll his cart inside but I stop him. "I've got it."

He nods before backing away.

"I love Hudson," Blossom squeals as she reaches for a strawberry and pops it into her mouth. She moans as she chews and my cock – already hard from watching her wander around the chalet with her silky smooth legs exposed – jerks.

"I'm going for a walk."

"What? It's raining."

"It's fine."

I reach for the door but she captures my wrist to stop me. "What's wrong, Jaxon? Shit. Are you hurt worse than you let on?"

She grabs my hand to examine it. She smooths her fingers over my knuckles. "The swelling has gone down and there's no bruising." She glances up at me from beneath her lashes. "Maybe your knuckles need a kiss to feel better."

She leans over to kiss my knuckles and her sleepshirt dips open offering me a view of her cleavage. Guessing by the smirk on her face, the little minx knows exactly what she's doing. She kisses each and every one of my knuckles.

"There. All better. Or is there somewhere else I need to kiss?"

I groan. "This is why I need to go for a walk."

Her brow furrows. "Are you avoiding me?"

"You're not making it easy for me to keep my hands to myself."

"Who said you have to keep your hands to yourself?"

I brush the hair from her face. "Our weekend is nearly over. On Monday, we'll return to our normal lives. And, as soon as Alan drops the lawsuit, we'll get an annulment."

Pain flashes into her eyes before she blinks and it's gone. Why would my words be painful to her? Maybe I saw wrong.

She grasps my shirt. "If this is over on Monday, why don't we enjoy one more night together?"

Because I'm afraid if I enjoy another night wrapped in her arms, I'm going to fall for her. Blossom is not the woman I thought she was. Yes, she's different than me. But she also doesn't run from her problems. She's wicked smart and understands my nerdy jokes – even joins in on them. And she never plans to leave my home of Smuggler's Hideaway.

"It's not a good idea."

She smiles and her eyes warm until they resemble a tawny whiskey. "I think it's an excellent idea."

"Blossom," I grumble.

"Grumbling at me is not helping the situation."

"What do you…" I trail off when I notice her nipples are hard. "You're making it awful hard for me to resist you."

She palms my cock and squeezes. "I get what you mean."

"You keep squeezing me and this will be over before it begins."

She freezes. "Begins? Do you mean…." She trails off with a wiggle of her brows.

I don't know why I bothered trying to resist this woman. She was irresistible before I realized how strong and fun she is.

After spending a weekend getting to know her better, I don't have a chance of resisting her.

"Clothes off. On the bed."

"Yes, sir. Right away, sir."

She's joking, but my cock doesn't realize it. It pounds in my pants, begging me to let it loose. I inhale a deep breath to get my body under control before I skip foreplay entirely.

I don't want this to be over too quickly. I want to take my time with Blossom. If this is our last time together, I want to memorize every inch of her. Taste every inch of her. Touch every inch of her.

She whips off her t-shirt and I moan at how hard her nipples are already. She bends over and shimmies out of her panties and I have to fist my hand before I smack her ass.

She climbs onto the bed and I take a second to memorize this moment. How her smile lights up her face. How a blush creeps from her cheeks down her long, elegant neck. How perky her breasts are. How shiny her skin is.

"Are you going to stare at me all night? Or are you going to touch me?"

"Watch it or all the action you'll get is me jacking myself off while I stare at your gorgeous body."

Her breath hitches. "Maybe later."

I shrug off my tuxedo jacket before ripping my bowtie off and unbuttoning my shirt. Blossom sits up in bed. "I like this show." She wolf whistles. "Take it all off."

I shake my head at how silly she is. I don't have enough silly in my life. My brothers are always goofing off but my life is serious. Until Blossom, I didn't realize I enjoyed silly.

I throw my shirt on top of my jacket before toeing off my shoes.

"I'm going to send a thank you letter to the rowers of America."

"The rowers of America?"

She motions to my chest. "To thank them for how sexy your shoulders and pecs are."

I chuckle. "If you want to thank anyone, thank Miles for wanting to surf before school and Eli and Rhett for insisting I watch him."

Her nose wrinkles. "I'm not thanking your brothers for how sexy you are."

I unzip my pants and let them fall to the floor before rolling the cart with champagne and strawberries toward the bed.

"You forgot something." She points to my briefs.

"They stay on for now."

She sticks her bottom lip out in a pout. "Are you going to make me wait?"

I nip her lip with my teeth. "Don't worry. You're going to enjoy this. Lay back down."

She doesn't hesitate to follow my orders. "Good girl."

She shakes her head. "Not a good girl. Just ready to get this show on the road. I've wanted to jump you since you punched Alan."

"I didn't realize you were this bloodthirsty."

"Neither did I. Until you punched my asshole ex in the nose." She shivers and I can't stop myself from reaching out to trace a finger along her side. She leans into my touch.

I pick up a strawberry and dip it in chocolate before placing the treat at her lips. She bites it and I swoop in to kiss her lips. She tastes of strawberries, chocolate, and something all Blossom. It's sweet and sexy and utterly irresistible.

"Can you handle messy?" I ask against her lips.

"I'm fine with messy. But are you?"

I shrug. "I guess we're about to find out."

I dip my finger into the chocolate to make sure it isn't too hot. Satisfied the liquid won't burn her skin, I drizzle the chocolate onto her breasts. She gasps before arching her back toward me. I take a mental picture. I want to remember this vision for the rest of my life.

I bend and lick the chocolate off her skin. I moan at the flavor of her skin combined with chocolate. The tart of cherries and the sweet of chocolate is a heady combination.

Once I've cleaned her skin, I reach for the chocolate again. This time, I pour it on her stomach. While I lick the chocolate, I play with her pretty breasts. I massage and knead her skin until she's writhing beneath me.

I lift my head to meet her gaze. "Something you need?"

"You," she breathes out. "I need you."

I smirk. "I'm right here."

"You're the smartest man I know, don't be obtuse. You know what I mean."

"I'm the smartest man you know?"

She grunts. "Do not get distracted. It wasn't a compliment. It was a mere statement of fact."

"If I'm the smartest man you know." I toy with her nipple. "I can probably do two things at once."

She arches her back in a silent plea for more. "We are not discussing the myth of multi-tasking while I'm naked in bed and aching for you."

"Aching for me?" I pinch her nipple and she moans.

"More, please."

I dip my fingers in chocolate before smearing it over her lips. She tries to lick it off but I capture her lips before she has the chance. I lay on top of her but prop myself on my elbows before I crush her as I devour her lips.

She gasps and I shove my tongue into her mouth. The chocolate is delicious, but it can't compare to the taste of Blossom. She's a unique flavor, I'm afraid I'm becoming addicted to.

She wraps her legs around my waist and rubs herself against my cock. My cock is hard and hot and I can't wait any longer. I shove my boxers down my thighs and notch myself at her entrance.

I inch inside. I moan at the feel of her walls surrounding me. Rippling around me. Nothing has ever felt better. No one has ever felt better.

I lift up to watch myself enter her and freeze. "Fuck."

"Yes, please."

"I forgot a condom."

I never forget a condom. Eli and Rhett drummed it into me from before the time I was interested in girls. Always protect yourself and her.

"It's okay. I'm on the pill and I haven't been with anyone since Alan."

I ignore the reference to Alan. I won't let her ex interfere with what is growing between Blossom and me.

Hold on. Growing between Blossom and me? Shit. So much for not falling for her.

"You trust me?"

She rolls her eyes. "I'm in this bed with you, aren't I? Of course, I trust you."

After everything Alan did – how he broke her trust, cheated on her, stole from her – she's willing to trust another man. I knew Blossom was strong. It's official. I'm falling for her.

"Hold on," I growl. "This is going to be hard and fast."

"Oh, goodie."

I slam into her and her fingernails dig into my shoulders. When I don't move, she wiggles underneath me.

"You promised hard and fast."

I inhale a deep breath to stop myself from coming after one thrust. This woman I'm falling for deserves more and she'll get it. She'll get everything I have to give.

Until Monday morning.

Chapter 26

BLOSSOM

I cuddle into the warmth surrounding me and inhale a deep breath. Ocean and whiskey. I'm addicted to the smell. And I'm becoming addicted to the man who carries the smell.

Too bad this all ends on Monday. My stomach sours but I ignore it. If I only have one more day with Jaxon, I'm not using the time to throw myself a pity party. I'm going to enjoy my last day with him.

Hold on. Why does today have to be our last day together? Why can't our relationship continue?

Yes, we agreed the marriage was fake when we said our vows on Friday. But I didn't expect to spend two nights getting sweaty in the sheets with Jaxon either. Maybe things have changed.

They certainly have for me. Before Friday, I was pissed at Jaxon for ghosting me. I'm no longer pissed.

Nope. I'm the idiot who's falling hard and fast for her fake husband. But who can blame me? He literally punched Alan to defend me. I would have never guessed my nerdy whiskey maker knew how to break someone's nose. Let alone that he'd actually break one at a wedding for me.

Jaxon kisses my ear. "What are you thinking so hard about?"

My stomach tingles at how gravelly his voice is in the morning. I want more of these mornings. But does he? Will he choose me, pick me? And do I have the courage to ask him?

"Not thinking. Just enjoying the morning." I guess I'm short on courage this morning.

"Liar. You always twirl a finger in your hair when you're thinking."

My hand freezes from where I am, in fact, twirling my hair.

"I don't always twirl my hair when I'm thinking."

He snorts. "I've watched you for the past months. I know you."

I rotate my body until I'm facing him. "You watched me? You ghosted me is more accurate."

He drops his chin but not before I notice the flush on his cheeks. "I thought it was for the best."

"For the best?" My brow wrinkles. How could ghosting someone ever be for the best?

"You're not on the island to stay. Mainlanders never stay."

"Mainlander?" I rear back. "I'm an islander now. I built a life here. I'm not going anywhere."

"I know. But I didn't a few months ago."

"Let me get this straight. You ghosted me because you thought I was only on Smuggler's Hideaway temporarily?"

"Yes."

"Liar."

His chin lifts and he glares at me. "I'm not lying."

"You certainly weren't telling the truth."

His eyes narrow on me. "Yes, I was."

"Okay. Prove it. Stare me in the eyes and tell me you ghosted me because you thought I was on the island temporarily."

His blue eyes gaze into mine. Shit. Was he telling the truth?

"Even if you stay on the island, it doesn't matter. We're too different."

"Too different?"

"You're outgoing and don't get scared to walk into a room full of people."

"I'm being punished for being an extrovert?"

"Not punished. You'll be bored of me in no time."

"Really?" I raise an eyebrow. "No other man has poured chocolate and champagne all over me before licking it off."

He frowns. "Most of the champagne ended up on the sheets."

I giggle. "I thought your face was going to burst into flames with how red it was when you phoned the reception to ask for new sheets."

"It's not nice to tease."

I snort. "You spent half the night teasing me."

He smirks. "Different kind of teasing."

My nipples perk up at the promise in his voice. "Why don't we continue this?" I ask before I realize what words were going to come out of my mouth.

"Continue what?"

The question is out there. I might as well fight for what I want. I motion between us. "Enjoying each other."

"Hooking up?"

I shrug. "Sure."

He shakes his head and my stomach sinks to my toes. He's saying no. He's not choosing me. He doesn't want me for more than a bit of fun on a weekend. I feel exposed and tighten the sheet around my naked body.

"I don't want a friends with benefits situation."

He doesn't … Hold on. We're speaking about two different things.

"I didn't mean friends with benefits."

He frowns as he reaches over me to snatch his glasses from the nightstand and put them on. "What did you mean?"

Holy smugglers. He's going to make me say the words.

"I enjoy how much chemistry we have between us. It's explosive and unlike anything I've ever experienced before." His nod is the encouragement I need to continue. "But I want to explore more than our chemistry. I want to get to know you. Spend time with you outside of the bedroom."

"As in dating and a relationship?"

"Yes," I agree and hold my breath as he contemplates his answer.

He fiddles with his glasses and I dig my fingers into my thighs to stop myself from throwing the glasses away and climbing on top of him to convince him to pick me. To give us a chance. But sex is not the way to convince Jaxon. He needs logic and reasoning.

"I've had a great time this weekend. Outside of this bed. At the rehearsal dinner Friday. The wedding yesterday. Even the dinner with those assholes who thought they were better than us was fun because I was with you."

"The dinner yesterday wasn't horrible."

"Until you punched the groom in the face."

"Alan deserved it."

"He's such an asshole. I can't believe I ever dated him. I can't believe my parents died worried I was with him. My parents died while I was rebelling against them." My eyes itch and I close them before any tears can escape.

Jaxon wraps an arm around me and pulls me near. "Don't cry. I don't know how to handle tears."

"You don't handle tears, nerd boy. You let the woman cry and hold her until she's finished."

His arm tightens around me. "Okay. Go ahead and cry. I will hold you until you're finished."

"You're not going to argue and tell me to get over it?"

"If this is what you need, I'll give it to you."

My body tingles at his words. Jaxon is not a man who would force me to go to my parents' funeral without him while whining, 'they never liked me'. He'd stand by my side. He'd hold my hand and not make me face the situation alone.

Damn. I want this man by my side for as long as he'll stay. Maybe forever.

"Thank you," I murmur.

He combs his fingers through my hair. "You never have to thank me for giving you what you need. But you may need to tell me what you need. I'm not exactly emotionally intelligent."

I tilt my head to meet his gaze. "Who said you're not emotionally intelligent? Do you want me to beat them up?"

He wipes the tears away from my cheeks. "We both know I'm going to suck at being in this relationship. I'm going to make all kinds of mistakes. Probably piss you off on a weekly basis."

"Wait a second. Are you saying you want to be in a relationship with me?"

He nods. "But you have to give me room to mess up."

"Same, nerd boy. Same."

He glares at me. "And you have to stop calling me nerd boy."

"What are you going to do about it?" I waggle my eyebrows. "Prove you're a man?"

"Are you finished crying?"

I nod.

"And you're no longer sad?"

"My tears have all dried up."

He contemplates me for a long moment before clearing his throat. "In which case, I will show you I'm a man."

He throws his glasses onto the side table before whipping the sheet off of me and crawling down the bed until he's kneeling between my legs.

"What are you doing?"

"I'm showing you I'm a man."

"I might have to call you boy more often."

He growls before shoving my legs further apart and settling his shoulders between my thighs. He pulls my lips apart with his fingers before latching onto my clit. I thread my hands through his hair and hold on tight.

Jaxon sucks on my clit as he sinks two fingers into me. He is not messing around. I am definitely teasing him about being a boy more often.

A memory of him ghosting me after we kissed tries to invade my mind but I ignore it. He explained why he ghosted me before. He won't do it again. I have faith in him.

Besides, if he tries to ghost me again, I'll sic his brothers on him.

And then I'll mend my broken heart. Because Jaxon ghosting me would hurt worse than Alan not accompanying me to my parents' wedding. Somehow, in one short weekend, he's lodged himself deeper into my heart than Alan ever managed.

Jaxon thrusts another finger into me and I forget all about the future. Allowing myself to enjoy this moment with him is not going to change our future anyway.

Chapter 27

"If it was possible to divorce your siblings, I would." ~ Jaxon

JAXON

I stifle a yawn as I swirl the whiskey mixture. I haven't been this tired since I was in college and decided I could handle twenty credits a semester. And I could handle seven classes during the semester. Surviving exam week was another matter entirely.

But I'm not exhausted from spending all night studying for an exam. I'm exhausted because I didn't get much sleep this weekend. Although Blossom and I spent all day Sunday in bed, there wasn't much sleep happening.

Blossom. The woman I'm now dating.

I frown. I don't know how to keep a vibrant, outgoing woman like her interested in me. Despite her reassurances, I worry she'll be bored of me and my simple life in record time. My heart stutters at the thought. It's entirely too attached to her already.

I rub a hand over my chest as I move to my computer. I click on the folder I created this morning.

The door bursts open and Kai, Zane, and Miles rush inside.

"Happy Friday!" Kai shouts.

"It's Monday."

He shrugs. "I refuse to be constrained by society's views on days and time."

"It's not society's views. Day and time is not a construct. A year is based on the Earth's revolution around the sun. Days and months are then—"

He whips up a hand to stop me. "Enough. I've heard your lectures before. It changes nothing. I don't care what day you call today. What I care about is how it's time to hit up the *Rumrunner* for drinks with your brothers."

I scowl. My younger brothers are always finding reasons to skip out on work. "I have work to do."

"Please, come with us," Kai pleads.

"Kai is anxious to visit *Rumrunner* since his girlfriend works there," Zane says.

Kai glares at him. "Harper is not my girlfriend."

Miles chuckles. "Not for lack of trying on your part."

"*How to Woo a Woman.*" Crap. While Kai and Miles were arguing, Zane crept up on me.

My brothers gather around my computer to read my screen. I try to click away from the book I was reading but Kai steals my keyboard and Zane, my mouse.

"Chapter one," Miles reads out loud. "Be chivalrous."

"Chivalrous?" Kai snorts. "What century was this book written in?"

Zane sighs. "And you wonder why Harper won't give you the time of day."

Kai glares at him. "As if you've been chivalrous a day in your life."

"Yeah." Miles nods in agreement. "Isn't your motto 'leave while they sleep'?"

Zane shrugs. "I always thank a woman before I leave. I don't wait for them to fall asleep."

This is exactly why I didn't ask my younger brothers for advice. Kai is hung up on an older woman who won't give him the time of day. And Zane and Miles are players.

And I'm not asking Rhett or Eli for advice. Eli stumbled and blushed through giving me the birds and bees talk. I waited until he was finished to let him know I'd already decided to wait until college for sex. I didn't wait, but since he believed I did, he left me alone.

"Chivalry isn't dead," Miles reads from my computer. "There's a list of examples of how to be chivalrous."

"Why do you need examples?" Kai asks.

"Yeah." Zane nods. "Aren't you married already?"

Miles elbows him. "It's fake, remember?" He whisper-shouts.

"Fake, right?" Kai winks. "The same way those scratches on his back on Saturday were fake."

I ignore how my back tingles and my balls tighten with memories of how I got those scratches. I can't get hard in front of my brothers. I'll never hear the end of it.

"Do none of you have work to do?" I ask.

Zane shrugs. "I can't do anything on the marketing campaign for the new flavor of whiskey until you figure out what it's going to be."

I find it difficult to believe the marketing manager of the distillery has nothing to do but as I have no clue what his actual duties are – marketing doesn't interest me in the least – I keep quiet.

"I did a couple of sales calls today. Sold a ton of whiskey. I deserve a break," Miles declares.

Whether he did sales calls or not is immaterial. Miles always thinks he deserves a break. Especially when the waves are 'off the hook' – whatever that means.

I cross my arms over my chest and address Kai. "I know you have work to do."

As the operations manager, Kai needs to be in the distillery the most often of my three younger brothers. Which is a problem since he's never on time and believes time is a construct to put the man down. I have no clue what that means either.

Kai's nose wrinkles. "The work never ends. If I stayed here until I was finished, I'd live here."

This is the reason I begged Eli to find an experienced operations manager for the distillery. Kai isn't mature enough for the position. I end up handling the majority of his tasks. I don't complain, though. It's easier to do the work than ask Kai to do it. He's an expert in making up excuses.

Rhett peers into my office. "I didn't know we were having a Raider brother meeting."

"We're not."

He motions to Miles, Zane, and Kai. "Four out of six brothers is a majority."

"They were just leaving."

Zane laughs. "He's trying to get rid of us because he doesn't want us to tell you what he's reading."

"Which is silly," Miles adds.

"Because, of course, we're telling you," Kai says.

Rhett crosses his arms over his chest and stares at our brothers. "Tell me what?"

"Nothing!" I shout as I snatch the keyboard from Kai and finally manage to shut the book I was reading.

"He's reading a book about how to woo a woman," Zane says.

I try to stop them but my cheeks warm with a blush.

"How to woo a woman?" Rhett asks and Zane nods. "This is great news."

Miles smirks. "Great fun, you mean."

Rhett waves a hand in dismissal at him. "Are you serious about Blossom?"

I contemplate lying. I don't want my brothers all up in my business. But there's little chance of them removing their noses from my business anytime soon. Besides, I don't want to keep Blossom a secret. I'm proud to be with her.

"We've agreed to start dating."

Kai's mouth drops open. "Say what now?"

Zane bumps his shoulder. "Don't be jealous because Harper won't date you."

"I'm not jealous," Kai mutters. "I'm surprised a woman as beautiful as—"

"Not to mention outgoing and fun," Miles interrupts to say.

"Would date Mr. Nerdy," Zane finishes.

My insecurities roar to life. They're right. Blossom is too different from me for this to work. I shouldn't have agreed to date her. She's going to end up breaking my heart.

Rhett squeezes my shoulder. "Don't listen to the rabble-rousers. They're trying to get a reaction out of you."

"After all, you do have a temper," Miles says.

I frown. "I do not have a temper."

He lifts an eyebrow. "And you didn't punch the groom in the face at a wedding either?"

"He deserved it."

"He deserved to have his nose broken?"

"Yes. He said some nasty things about Blossom. I asked him politely to stop. He refused. I felt consequences were necessary to make my point."

"I'm just going to say it," Zane says. "I'm loving my nerdy, emotionless brother falling in love."

It's true. I am falling in love. I'm helpless to stop the fall when it comes to Blossom. I did try. I attempted to ignore her for months. But Blossom is not a woman who can be ignored.

"I am not emotionless," I argue, since I'm not discussing how I feel about Blossom with my brothers.

"Obviously, since you punched Blossom's ex at his wedding."

I didn't suddenly develop emotions this weekend. But I refuse to argue this point with Zane or any of my other brothers. It's an argument I can't win. Trust me. I've tried. I know when to retreat with grace.

"Aren't you on your way to *Rumrunner*?" I try to shoo them out of my office.

Rhett growls. "No one better be on their way to a bar at two in the afternoon on a Monday."

Kai groans. "You're boring."

"You're lucky the waves aren't calling my name," Miles mutters as he leaves. Kai and Zane follow him out.

"Thanks," I tell Rhett.

"You can thank me later."

"Later?"

"After you fuck this up and I help you get your girl back."

I push my glasses on top of my head and massage the bridge of my nose. "You're not helping the situation."

He slaps me on the back. "I am. You don't realize it yet. But I am."

"Oh, there you are." Dakota enters the room. "You disappeared on me."

He throws his arm around her shoulders. "Sorry, Havoc. My brothers were having a meeting without me."

"The manager of *Velvet Blossom* phoned twice."

Velvet Blossom is a restaurant chain we supply with whiskey.

"Shit. I'll phone her now."

Rhett hurries away, but Dakota doesn't move. In fact, she shuts the door behind him.

"Is something wrong?"

"Are you dating Blossom?"

I'm surprised she doesn't know since Blossom is her best friend. Or maybe this is a trick question. I never did understand trick questions. "Yes."

"Finally."

"I'm done ghosting her."

"Good. She deserves better than a man who ghosts her."

"She does."

"I like the two of you together."

"So do I."

"But if you hurt her, I won't hesitate to pour vinegar in your vats of whiskey," she says with a glare before opening the door and strolling out of my office.

If I hurt Blossom, I'll deserve any wrath Dakota can dish out.

But I'm not worried about hurting Blossom. I will probably mess up since this is a new situation for me. But my mess ups won't be intentional. I'd never hurt Blossom on purpose.

And I don't think she'd hurt me on purpose. Except she thinks she won't get bored of me. I'm afraid she's wrong. And when she does get bored, it will hurt.

Chapter 28

"Wait a minute. Those people aren't smugglers." ~
Blossom

BLOSSOM

The doorbell rings and I yell, "Coming!"

I rush to the front door while putting on my shoe. I fling it open and smile at Jaxon. "Hi."

He shoves a bunch of flowers into my arms. "These are for you."

I lift the bouquet to my nose and inhale their scent. They smell of spring and new beginnings. "Thank you. I thought tulips were out of season."

"I ordered them."

"But shouldn't they take a week to get here?"

He shrugs. "I did a rush order."

I can only imagine how much a rush order would cost. I slap him with the flowers – gently, I'm not ruining these beauties. "No more spending ridiculous amounts of money on me."

"I'm trying to woo you."

I start to laugh but sober when I realize he's serious. Jaxon Raider wants to woo me? Who am I to stand in his way?

I quickly put the flowers in water and Jaxon leads me outside. When we pass his Mustang, I stop.

"Aren't we driving? We can hardly steal a Smuggler's Hide-away mascot without a car."

He frowns. "Steal a mascot?"

"Rhett took Dakota to steal the parrot mascot from Pirate's Perch on their first date."

Each town on Smuggler's Hideaway has a live mascot. Smuggler's Rest has Viking – the cutest otter ever. Pirate's Perch has Plank – the dirty-mouthed parrot. And Rogue's Landing has Rogue – the chaos-causing raccoon.

His frown deepens. "Is that what you want to do? Steal Plank?"

"You need to do something. You're losing the prank war."

"How do you know I'm in a prank war with my brothers?"

"Dakota told me."

"I haven't thought of a prank yet."

I wrap my arm around his bicep. "No need to think any further. We could steal Viking. I know where he is."

"Everyone on the island knows Parker has the otter. We usually rotate who's watching the mascot, but Parker refuses to give him up."

"I can't blame her. Otters are adorable. And Viking is so cute. He gives cuddles for cookies."

He sighs. "I thought Dakota was the otter lover."

I shrug. "He's too cute not to love."

"I made a reservation at *Smuggler's Cove* but I can cancel it and we can go steal Viking instead."

I bounce on my toes. "No way. It's the *Smuggler's Reenactment Dinner* week. I've been dying to go, but the tickets were sold out before I even moved to the island."

He smirks. "Good thing I have connections."

"Why are you dragging your feet?" I say when he doesn't quicken his steps to match mine.

"Why are you in such a hurry? I thought we'd have a nice stroll before dinner."

I wrinkle my nose. "Is this part of the wooing thing?"

He grunts. "I'm trying to be romantic."

I push up on my toes and kiss his cheek. "You bought tickets to an event I've wanted to attend since I learned about it. You're getting straight As for this date thus far."

He blows out a breath. "Good. I want you to have fun."

I frown. I was joking, but he's obviously not.

"I'm having fun because I'm with you." The doubt in his blue eyes slays me. "I'm serious, nerd boy. I enjoy your company."

He meets my gaze for a long moment. "What did I say about calling me nerd boy?"

"You can punish me later." I wink.

"You're trouble, Petal."

"I'm not the one who wasted a good bottle of champagne."

"You thoroughly enjoyed the champagne."

I shiver at the deep tone of his voice. I certainly did enjoy myself as he licked the champagne off my naked body. I should add champagne to my shopping list.

We arrive at *Smuggler's Cove* and he opens the door for me.

"I like the chivalrous act."

"Not an act."

I smile up at him. "Even better."

He places a hand on my lower back and leads me to the hostess. "Hello, Hazel. We have a reservation."

"Oh, hi Jaxon. I didn't expect to see you here."

He squeezes my hip. "Blossom wanted to come."

She offers me her hand. "I'm Hazel. Good on you for snagging the one remaining Raider brother."

My brow furrows. "There are three other single Raider brothers."

She rolls her eyes. "Miles, Zane, and Kai are children. Especially Miles," she mutters. "Let me show you to your table."

"No menu?" I ask once we're seated in the middle of the restaurant.

"It's a set menu," she says before walking off to help another customer.

I lean over the table. "You have to tell me what the deal is."

Jaxon pushes his glasses up his nose. "The deal?"

"Why Hazel hates Miles."

"Oh. That deal. Hazel and Miles used to date. He dumped her before he flew off for a surfing competition in Hawaii."

"What an asshole! Sorry." I immediately backpedal. "He's your brother. I shouldn't be saying he's an asshole." I throw my fist in the air. "Go Raider brothers!"

He chuckles as he catches my hand. "You can make fun of Miles as much as you want."

I narrow my eyes. "Really? Or is this a trick?"

"What kind of trick would this be?"

I forgot Jaxon doesn't play games. "Never mind."

The door to the restaurant bangs open and someone shouts, "The bootleggers are here!"

"Oh, goodie." I rub my hands together. "The show is about to begin."

A woman rushes into the restaurant and a man chases after her. They aren't dressed as bootleggers, but maybe the whole point is bootleggers were everyday people? I don't know.

"Those aren't bootleggers," Jaxon whispers.

"You know who they are?"

He doesn't have a chance to answer before the man and woman arrive at our table.

"Jaxon Raider! How could you!" The woman yells before bursting into tears.

What is going on? Who is this woman? And why is she mad at Jaxon? She can't possibly be dating him. She's old enough to be his mother. His mother? Hold on. Is this his mom?

Jaxon stands. "Do we have to do this now?"

"Did you get married and not tell your mom?" The man's question confirms my suspicions. These people are his parents. I am not ready to meet the parents, but I don't run away from my problems either.

I stand next to Jaxon. "I'm Blossom."

Hazel hurries to us. "There's a private dining room you can use. Unless you want everyone in the restaurant to eavesdrop on your private business."

We follow her to the back of the restaurant. Everyone stares at us as we make our way past the tables. I wave to them. Let them think we're part of the entertainment.

"Mom," Jaxon pleads once we're shut behind a closed door in a private room. "Let me explain."

"No, I'll explain. This is my fault."

His mom's eyes widen before her gaze drops to my belly. "Am I going to be a grandmother? How exciting. Your child and Eli's child will grow up together."

"Eli's child?" Jaxon asks.

"Oops. I'm not supposed to tell anyone."

His father chuckles. "Except you just told Jaxon and his wife that Paisley's pregnant."

"Hold on!" I raise a hand. "Paisley's pregnant? No way. She would have told me. I'm her assistant. I need to prepare for her absence."

Jaxon's mom gasps as she reaches for my hand. "It's true. You are married. This is a beautiful ring." She smiles at Jaxon. "Good job, son."

My nose wrinkles. "You don't think the ring is too big? It's a bit ostentatious, isn't it?"

She giggles. "I love her already."

I'm confused. "What did I say?"

"There have been some issues with women throwing themselves at Eli for his money," Jaxon explains.

I narrow my eyes on his parents. "I don't mean any disrespect but Paisley loves Eli. She is not with him for his money."

His mom claps. "You're wonderful. Welcome to the family."

She opens her arms as if to hug me but Jaxon growls. "Don't scare her."

"Why would a hug scare me? I'm a strong woman. I can handle a hug."

Jaxon fiddles with his glasses. "I just thought… since you lost your mom… and the crying…"

I throw my arms around him. "You better stop being sweet, nerd boy, or I am never letting you go."

"Who said I wanted you to let me go?" he whispers into my ear and I melt into him. This man I'm falling for doesn't want to let me go. Maybe he'll choose me after all.

"Son," his father grumbles. "Properly introduce us to your wife."

"And then explain why we weren't invited to the wedding."

I release Jaxon but he wraps an arm around my waist to keep me near. Protecting me again. I want to argue I don't need protecting, but I'm enjoying his warmth too much to care about asserting my independence.

"Mom, Stuart, this is Blossom."

"Stuart?" I ask. "You call your dad by his name?"

"Stuart is my step-dad."

"Step-dad?"

"My biological father left when I was fourteen."

No wonder Jaxon never mentions his father. I have at least a million questions about what happened but I'm not asking them in front of his parents.

"It's nice to meet you, Ms. Raider and Stuart."

"You can call me Jessica. Or Mom if you prefer."

"Mom," Jaxon growls.

I pat his arm. "It's okay."

"I'm still waiting to hear why you got married without your mom in attendance," Jessica pushes.

Jaxon sighs. "It's Blossom's personal business."

"It's okay." I blow out a breath. "In short, my ex is trying to steal half of the inheritance I received when my parents died."

"What?" Stuart booms his question loud enough for all of the people in the restaurant to hear. Closed doors be damned.

"You lost your parents?" Jessica asks as she wipes tears from her eyes.

"Two years ago."

"I don't understand how marrying Jaxon can help your situation but if Jaxon married you to help, it'll help. All of my boys are saviors."

"We should let the kids have their dinner," Stuart says.

"But I have more questions," Jessica complains. Stuart stares at her until she huffs. "Fine. But I expect to see you at Sunday dinners since you're part of the family now."

"The marriage isn't real," I remind her.

She rolls her eyes. "I'll see you soon."

Stuart escorts her out of the room and I stare after them. Jessica accepted me into the family without a second thought. No games. No tests. Just acceptance.

My chest warms. Family. I haven't had one of those in a while. I hope I can keep this one.

Chapter 29

"I did warn you." ~ Jaxon

JAXON

I drum my fingers on the table in my office. This new flavor profile for the whiskey *Buccaneer's* is planning to debut for the holidays isn't working. I don't know where I went wrong.

I carefully selected the grains. I combined them for a unique flavor. I kept a close eye on the fermentation process. After much consideration, I decided which portion of the distillation to use in the final product. I used a bourbon cask and regularly checked on the aging whiskey.

The blending has to be the problem. I've tried different barrels and batches of whiskey to finely tune the final product but I'm not there yet. This whiskey should give the drinker a taste of Christmas spices, ginger, coffee, and dark chocolate. A rich yet balanced taste that goes down smooth at a holiday dinner.

But it doesn't.

I scan the table. It's covered in various whiskey samples as well as my notes from each blending attempt. I gather the notes together. I will carefully review them to figure out the issue.

Once I've disposed of these blends, I'll start over.

The door bangs open and slams into the wall. "What the hell, Jaxon?"

I frown at Blossom. She can't possibly be upset I'm pouring whiskey away. She knows enough about whiskey distilling to understand I'm not wasting the whiskey. Unlike my brothers who think any liquid from the barrels is drinkable. It's not.

"These are the blends I didn't approve."

She fists her hands on her hips. "I don't give a shit about the whiskey."

"You're angry?"

"What was your first clue?"

"The door banging open."

She shakes her head. "I wasn't being literal."

I grimace at yet another example of my social awkwardness. "Sorry."

"Don't be sorry. Answer your phone."

I'm getting more confused as this conversation progresses. "Sorry?"

Her nostrils flare. "Stop saying sorry."

"I'm sorry." She growls. "Sorry. I didn't mean to…" I trail off and inhale a deep breath. "I don't understand what's happening. Why are you mad?"

She points at the clock.

"It's seven p.m.," I read.

"And?"

"And…" I search my mind for why she would be angry at me for working at seven p.m. I work late most days. She knows this. Except for when I have plans.

"Oh shit," I mutter when I remember. "We were going to dinner."

"And you forgot."

"I'm sorry."

"Enough with sorry! It's bad enough you forgot we were having dinner today but you didn't answer any of my texts. I was worried. I didn't know if you were hurt. If something happened. If you were lying dead in a ditch with your face being eaten off by a seal."

I open my mouth to tell her seals don't eat human faces but then I notice her sniff and a tear leaks from her eye. Her tears slay me. Fortunately, I know what to do because she taught me how to handle this situation. I wrap her in my arms and sway her from side to side.

"I'm so sorry, Petal. I didn't think. I always switch my phone on silent when I work. I didn't hear your messages."

She fists my t-shirt. "You don't know how it feels to get a call telling you the worst has happened."

I wipe her tears from her cheeks. "I wish you didn't know how it feels either."

"But I do."

Her eyes, normally a brilliant whiskey brown, are red and puffy. It breaks my heart to see her this way.

"Tell me how to make you feel better."

She smiles but it doesn't light up her face the way it usually does. "You can't make it better. I'm grieving their loss. I'll probably always grieve the loss of my parents."

I nod. I understand. I grieve the loss of my father. Except he's not dead. He's a mainlander, who ditched the island, leaving my mom to raise six children on her own.

"Is this one of those situations when chocolate and wine helps?"

"One of those situations?"

I shrug. "I've been researching how to be a good partner."

"You have?"

My cheeks warm but I ignore them. "I thought it would help me make less mistakes. I guess I need to research more since I messed up today."

She grasps my hands. "You messed up but it's okay. No one's perfect, although I am pretty close."

I grin. "Yes, you are."

This time, when she smiles, it does light up her face. "It's good you realize how perfect I am now."

I can't resist those lips. I meld my mouth to hers. She sighs and I thrust my tongue inside. Her taste of cherries hits me, and I growl before pulling her near until her chest hits mine.

I palm her neck and tilt her head so I can dive deeper into the kiss. I want to explore every inch of her mouth. I want to memorize her taste. I want her taste on my tongue.

I grasp her hips and place her on the table. She wraps her legs around me. My cock – already hard and heavy – presses against my zipper in an effort to reach her.

In one weekend, we had more sex than I did with my previous girlfriend over a six-month period. And yet, I can't get enough of her. I'm afraid I never will.

I thread my hand through her hair before gathering it at her nape and tugging to expose her neck to me. I nibble and lick my way down her neck until I reach the junction with her shoulder, where I bite down.

Blossom moans as her legs tighten around my waist and her fingernails dig into my arms.

"I love your cherry taste," I murmur against her skin. I draw a finger along her neck and shoulder and enjoy watching the goosebumps explode in my wake.

"Cherry?"

"Mh-hum. Cherry."

I love the taste of cherries. Sweet with a slight hint of tart. It would be a great addition to any whiskey. Aha! It's what's missing. I snap my head up. "That's it!"

Blossom gazes at me with dazed eyes. "What's it?"

"Cherry. It's the missing flavor."

"I still don't understand. You're going to have to explain more, nerd boy."

"The flavor profile for the new whiskey. I couldn't figure out what was missing. It's why I was lost in concentration and forgot the time."

Forgot the time. Shit. Going complete nerdy whiskey distiller on Blossom is not the way to her heart.

"Never mind." I pull her close again. "Forget I said anything."

She presses a hand on my chest to create space between us. "I won't forget you said anything. I want to understand."

"But we were making out and I thought of my whiskey."

She grins. "In other words, I inspired the whiskey."

"You did." I reach for my notes. "I've been working on a new flavor profile for a holiday whiskey all day but I couldn't get it right. It was missing something."

"Cherry?"

I nod. "Exactly."

"But how do you add cherry taste to whiskey. You're not going to add actual cherries, are you?" Her nose wrinkles in distaste and I tweak it.

"No, I am not. I have something better."

"Don't leave me hanging."

I pause. "You're serious? You're interested."

"Duh." She rolls her eyes. "Have you met me? Chemical engineering degree and aspiring brewer who begged you for a tour of the distillery."

"Sometimes I forget how smart you are."

She frowns. "You forgot I'm a genius? Rude."

I comb the hair from her face. "I'm used to smart girls who are similar to me."

"Sexy? You don't think I'm sexy?"

"Will you stop twisting my words?"

"Sorry. I'll do anything for you but I can't do that."

"Are you quoting Meatloaf?"

"Would a smart and sexy woman like me listen to Meatloaf?"

I realize I've talked myself into a corner and give up. "I bought a few barrels from a cherry liquor producer a while back. I'm going to transfer the whiskey to those barrels for a finishing period. It will add a subtle cherry-like character."

"It'll add a complex flavor. Brilliant idea. For which I take the credit."

I chuckle. "Naturally."

"What are you waiting for? Let's get to work."

"You're going to help?"

She narrows her eyes. "You better not say I can't help because I'm a woman. Those are fighting words."

"No. I..." I clear my throat. "I didn't expect you to be this interested in the process."

"You don't get it, do you?"

"Get what?"

"I'm interested in whatever you're doing. You are interesting to me."

I study her brown eyes for any hint of deception. I don't understand how this woman could possibly be interested in me. I'm a nerd who – according to my brothers – has the social skills of a sea cucumber.

But there's no deception to be found in Blossom's gorgeous eyes. She's being genuine. She's interested in me. My boring life doesn't feel boring with her in it.

No wonder I'm falling for this woman. She's not only perfect. She's perfect for me.

Chapter 30

"Note to self. Always bring an umbrella if you're meeting the Raider brothers." ~ Blossom

BLOSSOM

"We don't have to go if you don't want to," Jaxon says as he drives toward his parents' house for Sunday lunch.

I gasp. "Of course, I want to go. How else am I going to learn all the embarrassing stories about you as a child?"

He frowns. "You won't learn them from my mom or Stuart."

My brow wrinkles. "I get Stuart didn't come into your life until recently but surely your mom has some juicy stories about you getting caught trying to sneak into the house after being out all night with your girlfriend. How about the time you came home drunk and threw up all over the front porch after trying Smuggler's Hideaway moonshine for the first time?"

"I've never thrown up on the front porch before."

"Aha! But you do admit to throwing up after the first time you tried Smuggler's Hideaway moonshine."

He grimaces. "Everyone throws up after the first time they try Smuggler's Hideaway moonshine."

"I didn't."

He glances over at me. "Really?"

"Yep." I grin. "Paisley forced me to drink a gallon of water after each shot of moonshine. I had to pee every thirty minutes for two days but I didn't throw up."

"Two days? The liquid should have—"

I place a finger over his lips to stop him. "Exaggeration was for entertainment purposes."

"I understand." He captures my hand and places it on his thigh. "My brothers are excellent at exaggeration."

"Do you get together every Sunday at your mom's house?"

"Not every Sunday."

What I wouldn't do to have a mom's house to gather at every Sunday with my siblings. But Jaxon's face reminds me of a convict on his way to the death chair.

"Can I ask why you don't want to go?"

"I didn't say I don't want to go."

"You didn't have to. Your face says it all."

He sighs. "It's not that I don't want to spend time with my family. But I'm worried what prank my brothers are going to try and pull since we're in the middle of this prank war."

My brow wrinkles. "Your mom is okay with them playing pranks at her house?"

"Mom can't complain."

"What do you mean? In my experience, moms can always complain."

"Forget I said anything."

"Nope. I am not forgetting anything."

"We're almost there."

I motion to a side street. "Pull over and explain yourself."

He scowls but does as I said and pulls over. He drums his fingers on the steering wheel for a few long seconds before finally admitting, "I don't want to disparage my mother. Not in front of you considering your history."

I grasp his hand to stop the drumming. "Jaxon, I…"

I cut myself off when I realize I nearly said I love him. I don't love Jaxon. Am I falling for him? Yes, I admit I am. But I haven't known him long enough to love him.

I clear my throat and try again without dropping any accidental love bombs. "You can say whatever you want or need to say about your mom or dad or brothers or the ghost of Smuggler's Hideaway. I don't want you to hold back from sharing with me because of my past. How am I supposed to get to know my husband if you hold back?"

"Ghost of Smuggler's Hideaway?"

I shrug. "There must be a ghost somewhere on this island." I squeeze his hand. "Stop stalling. Tell me what's bothering you."

He blows out a breath. "Nothing in particular is bothering me."

I raise an eyebrow.

"It's just… Well, Mom throws these Sunday meals for us every month as if we're this tight-knit family, but while I was growing up, she was never around."

"Why was she never around?"

He lifts his glasses up and pinches the bridge of his nose. "Dad left us when I was fourteen. We had this great party for Eli's sixteenth birthday at Prohibition Beach, but two days later, he was gone and never returned."

"What an asshole."

"We never heard from him again, which left Mom all alone to raise six kids by herself."

My nose wrinkles. "He never paid any child support?"

He purses his lips. "No. He disappeared. Mom worked two jobs, but it wasn't enough. So, Eli got odd jobs to help her pay for the bills, and Rhett helped out with raising us since Mom was never around."

From what I've seen, Eli and Rhett are still looking out for their younger brothers. Eli founded the distillery for them, and Rhett tries to keep them in line. He fails. But he does try.

"To sum up, you feel you're not a close-knit family because everyone in the family pulled together when you were a teenager to make certain there was food on the table and homework was done."

He groans. "You make me sound like an asshole."

"No. No. No." I squeeze his hands. "I'm merely pointing out there's a good reason why your mom wasn't around when you were a teenager. Sometimes the memory of our hearts doesn't align with the memory of our mind."

"What?"

"Your heart remembers your mom not being around. Even though your mind knows she wasn't around for damn good reasons, your heart doesn't let you forget about how much you missed your mom."

"Huh. This is a very good way of explaining it."

"I'm glad you approve. I'll write my therapist a thank-you note."

"You have a therapist?"

I roll my eyes. "Duh. My parents died in a car accident on their way to visit me for Christmas because my husband refused to visit them. I've been paying the guilt police ever since."

"You can't blame yourself. It was an accident."

"My mind knows this. My heart doesn't."

His mouth drops open. "Oh."

"Hold on." I dig around in my purse.

"What are you doing?"

"Taking a picture of the moment I rendered Jaxon Raider, the brilliant master whiskey distiller, speechless."

"You think you're funny."

"Wrong." I giggle. "I know I'm funny."

He palms my neck and draws me near until our lips meet. His scent of whiskey and ocean and something undeniably Jaxon surrounds me and I sink into the kiss. Our tongues meet and we duel for supremacy.

Jaxon growls and his hand on my neck squeezes as he deepens the kiss. I dig my—

Honk! A car whizzes past and blares its horn at us, startling us apart.

Jaxon's glasses are all fogged up and his face is soft as he smiles at me. There's no denying it. I am totally falling for this man who struggles to understand his emotions.

My phone alarm beeps. "We're late."

He chuckles. "You are obsessed with time."

I shrug. "I make no apologies."

He puts the car into gear and we drive the remainder of the way to his parents' house. He glances around as he parks in the driveway.

"What's wrong?"

"None of my brothers are here."

"Is it a problem if they aren't here?"

"My mother will ask you a million questions."

I pat his hand. "Don't worry. If I can handle her nerdy son, I can handle her."

I open the car door and—

Splat!

A water balloon hits my chest and explodes.

"First point for me!" Kai shouts.

Jaxon shoves me behind him. "No throwing water balloons at my wife."

"We're pranking you," Zane says.

"This isn't a prank," Jaxon declares.

"Why not?" Miles asks. "We shocked you and Blossom."

"Surprising us is not a practical joke."

Zane smirks. "But it is mischievous."

Jaxon sighs. "I'm never going to win this prank war."

Wrong. He has me on his side now. I'll help him win the prank war with his brothers *and* show him it's okay to have fun. You can be a serious person with a serious job and still have fun. Life doesn't have to be about work all the time.

Jaxon doesn't realize how lucky he is to have married me.

He lifts his t-shirt up to wipe water from his face and exposes miles and miles of toned, tanned skin. Correction. I'm the lucky one.

Chapter 31

BLOSSOM

"Why do you want to go to the distillery?" Jaxon asks as we drive away from my apartment. "I thought you were hungry."

"We'll go to dinner afterwards. For now, I have the best idea." I nearly cackle. Jaxon is going to win the prank war with the Raider brothers because of this prank. It is the best!

"About the holiday whiskey? I've been working on calculations for how long we should keep the blend in the cherry casks."

"Nope. I have another idea."

"Another blend?"

I giggle. "Not everything in the world is about whiskey, nerd boy."

He mock growls at me. "I proved to you I'm not a boy."

I bat my eyelashes. "Maybe I forgot and need you to prove it again."

"You're such a troublemaker."

"Just wait until you see what I have planned for tonight."

His cheeks warm and he squirms in his seat. "I don't think we should have sex in my office again."

"Why not?"

"Because you broke all my test vials."

"Me?" I point to myself. "I broke all the test vials?"

"I misspoke. *We* broke all the test vials."

I pat his arm. "Don't worry. We can have sex in your car instead."

He glances over at me with his mouth gaping open. "You want to have sex in the car?"

I shrug. "I've never had sex in a car before."

"You—"

"Watch out!" I point to the road. "Sammy's in the street."

The brakes squeal and my seatbelt pulls tight as we come to a screeching halt. I realize I closed my eyes and open them. I scan the road but there's no sign of the seal.

"Oh no. I can't see Sammy." I fiddle with my seatbelt but can't get it unlocked. Jaxon reaches over and clicks it open for me. I rush outside.

"Sammy!"

The seal barks and I fall to my knees in front of him. Jaxon's Mustang is mere feet from where he's lying in the road.

"You can't lay in the middle of the road near a curve, Sammy boy."

If seals could roll their eyes, Sammy would be rolling his at me now. He does what he wants, when he wants. His attitude is not helped by tourists who now visit Smuggler's Hideaway to catch glimpses of him. There's even an app for 'spotting' the seal.

Jaxon kneels next to me. "I'm sorry, Sammy. I got distracted." He nods to me. "Look at her. She's beautiful. It's hard not to get distracted when she's near."

He honks and wags his tail as if he's in agreement with Jaxon.

"And you call me a troublemaker." I shake my head. "Calling me beautiful to divert attention from your lack of paying attention to the road. Tsk. Tsk."

Jaxon palms my neck to draw me near. "You are beautiful, Petal. Have I not told you enough?"

"You can never tell a woman she's beautiful too often."

"Duly noted," he whispers as his head descends toward mine.

"Honk! Honk!"

I startle and fall on my ass at Sammy's honking. "The seal doesn't approve of us making out in the middle of the road."

Jaxon stands and offers me a hand. "He's probably correct. We should move the car before there's an accident."

"Get off the road, Sammy." Naturally, the seal doesn't move. He's stubborn. "Don't make me call the dog catchers on you." Threatening to call the dog catchers is the only surefire way to get the stubborn seal to move.

He growls before galumphing off. Once he's off the road, we return to the car.

"Do you want me to wear a veil so I don't distract your driving with my beauty?" I ask as Jaxon starts to drive.

"And you wonder why I call you a troublemaker."

I giggle. He's going to think I'm a huge troublemaker after tonight.

We arrive at the distillery and he parks. But when he goes to open his door, I stop him.

"I should probably tell you what we're doing here."

He pushes his glasses up his nose. "It would make things easier."

"I have the best prank idea for you to win the prank war with your brothers."

He raises a brow. "Tell me."

I lift the large bag I prepared. "We're going to shut down the distillery."

"Shut down the distillery?"

"Yep. The Island Environmental Protection Authority is halting operations due to the distillery fatally disrupting a nesting site for the Spectacled Dune Crab."

"There is no Island Environmental Protection Authority, and the Spectacled Dune Crab doesn't exist."

I pull a crab shell out of my bag. "There isn't?"

He chuckles. "What's the plan?"

"I have government seizure notices, yellow tape to bar entry to the building, and crab shells as evidence."

"I'm finally going to win the prank war."

"Wrong. *We're* going to win the prank war."

He presses a quick kiss to my lips. "You're perfect, Petal."

My heart thuds in my chest. Does this man, who I'm falling for, seriously think I'm perfect? I bite my tongue before I can blurt out how much I love him.

I don't love him. I'm falling for him. Two entirely different things.

Except when I gaze into his blue eyes, I realize I'm no longer falling. I've fallen. I love this man. This nerdy, whiskey obsessed, socially awkward man is the person I want to spend the rest of my life with.

Jaxon brushes the hair from my forehead. "Is something wrong?"

Besides, my terror he won't choose me? Nope. No problem at all. I force a smile. "Why would anything be wrong?"

"You look like you saw a ghost."

"Just imagining the sweet, sweet victory when we surprise your brothers."

I jump out of the car before he can question me more. I'm afraid if he asks too many questions, I'll confess my love. Which would be a fool move. We've barely started dating. He'd hide in his lab with the door locked and barricaded if I declared my love this early.

"I'm thinking the official notice on the door to the offices along with some yellow tape. We'll put more yellow tape on the garage door entrance to the distillery, along with some crab shells scattered on the ground."

Once I've explained my plan, we get to work. I'm putting the finishing touches on the crab shell 'evidence' when I hear a car pull up. I glance over my shoulder. Shit. Eli's massive SUV is parking next to Jaxon's Mustang.

"We're busted!" I throw the extra yellow tape and crab shells in my bag before rushing to Jaxon and grasping his hand. "We came back to the distillery because you had another brilliant idea inspired by me of course and noticed the signs."

Eli and Paisley approach and I squeeze Jaxon's hand. "Stick to our story."

"What are you…" Eli trails off when another car turns into the parking lot.

Who now? This is ridiculous. The one night I decide to prank the distillery all of the Raider brothers show up. Well, not all. I do have one ace in the hole. As in Dakota is keeping Rhett away.

Miles, Zane, and Kai pile out of the second car and make their way to where we're gathered.

"What's going on?" Kai asks.

"What are you doing here? Is there a problem?" Jaxon asks. Oh, he's good. Going on the attack.

"Kai said you were throwing out good whiskey," Zane answers.

Miles grins. "And we're here to drink it."

Jaxon scowls. "I'm not throwing out whiskey."

Kai points at him. "I saw you."

Jaxon crosses his arms over his chest. "I do not throw out whiskey."

"What are you doing here?" I ask Paisley.

"We were … um…" She stutters as her cheeks darken.

"They were here to recreate the night she got pregnant," Miles answers.

Eli growls. "How do you know?"

He smirks. "I didn't. But I do now."

"I'm hungry," I announce in an overly loud voice. "You promised me dinner, Jaxon."

"What's this?" Eli asks before Jaxon can respond. He rips the notice off of the office door. "We're being shut down by the Island Environmental Protection Authority for fatally disrupting a nesting site for the Spectacled Dune Crab?"

Miles, Zane, and Kai rush to Eli.

"What the hell is going on? What's a Spectacled Dune Crab?" Zane asks.

Kai kneels down and picks up one of the shells. "I'm guessing it's a plastic crab."

"Plastic?" Miles snatches the shell from Kai. "What's going on?"

"Now I know why you wanted to borrow my laminating machine today," Paisley mutters.

I glare at her. "You're cheating."

"There is no cheating in a prank war."

"You weren't supposed to show up to have sex with Eli in his office."

She shrugs. "Pregnancy hormones have a significant effect on my libido."

Kai pushes his way in between us. "Hold on. Prank war? This was a prank?"

Eli waves the notice. "The government seizure notice refers to the shut down of a distastery and not a distillery."

Miles rips the yellow tape off the door. "And the tape says *Party Zone – Caution: Dancing Ahead* on the back."

Zane holds up his phone. "And I found the Pinterest board Blossom made of prank ideas."

"Good attempt, Jaxon, but you're still losing the prank war," Kai says.

I scowl. "I should at least get some credit for the effort I put into this prank."

Kai shakes his head at Jaxon. "You forced your wife to think of a prank for you?"

"He didn't force me. I came up with this idea. Which would have worked if Eli wasn't horny and you lot didn't want to drink free whiskey."

Miles throws his arm around my shoulders. "I, for one, think Blossom did an awesome job."

"Thank you."

"But you're still losing the prank war, little sis." He winks.

Little sis? My heart nearly gallops out of my chest. I would love to have a bunch of brothers. Any family, really.

"Welcome to the family," Kai adds.

"Welcome to the zoo is more like it," Zane mutters, but guessing by the sparkle in his eyes, he loves this particular zoo.

I think I'm going to love it, too. Brothers and a man I love – what more could a girl who's lost her parents want?

Chapter 32

"I never want to see a ball of paint again." ~ *Jaxon*

JAXON

"Are you ready?" I ask when Blossom opens her door.

Her smile stretches from ear to ear. "Ready to kick some Raider ass."

"Except mine, I hope."

"If you're on the opposite team, I make no promises."

I haul her near and kiss the smile off of her face. By the time I'm done exploring her mouth, her eyes are glazed over and her lips are swollen.

"Still going to kick my ass?"

"Sounds kinky but okay."

I grin as I lead her to my car. I never thought I'd enjoy having a sassy woman, but I enjoy all of Blossom's traits – sassy or otherwise.

"Have you been to the *Glowin' Galleon* before?" I ask as I start driving out of Smuggler's Rest toward the paintball arena.

"I wish. Dakota refuses to go with me. Apparently, I'm too 'competitive'."

I grin at her use of air quotes. "Maybe because you threatened to sell your horse to the glue factory if he didn't hurry up when you were at *Sirens & Saddles.*"

She gasps and clutches her chest. "You lie!" I raise an eyebrow at her and she huffs. "I said, 'don't make me threaten you'. It's not the same as actually threatening."

"Sure, it's not."

"Who will be there today?" she asks and I cringe. "What's wrong? Why are you cringing? Is your ex-girlfriend coming? Annoying, but I can hardly complain since you accompanied me to the wedding of my ex."

I reach across the console and squeeze her thigh. "No ex is coming, but you should probably know this is a family day."

She rolls her eyes. "Because you're losing the prank war. I get it."

"We're going to *Glowin' Galleon* because I'm losing the prank war, but me losing is not the reason we're getting together today."

"Spit it out. What's going on? Are Eli and Paisley getting married? I am so jealous. I want to get married on a pirate ship."

"I thought you wanted to get married on the beach."

"I didn't realize a pirate ship was an option."

"A pirate ship with people running around shooting each other with paint is your idea of an ideal wedding location?"

Her nose wrinkles. "I didn't consider the paintball. It would ruin a wedding dress."

"And running around chasing people with a paintball gun without shoes on would be rough."

"I guess this means Eli and Paisley aren't getting married."

"No. It's my birthday."

"What?" Blossom screeches. "It's your birthday and you didn't tell me? We're dating, Jaxon. This is information you share with the woman you're dating." She slaps my shoulder. "I can't believe you. I haven't had the chance to buy you a present. I'm showing up at your birthday party without a gift."

I capture her hand and squeeze. "You don't need to give me a present. Your presence is all I need."

It's true. Blossom is all I need. She's the woman I'm falling for. The woman I want to spend all my time with. I've never been distracted at work before – I have excellent skills of concentration – but I find myself staring into space, wondering what she's doing at random times during the day.

She lifts our hands to kiss my knuckles. "Good save, nerd boy. Good save."

I pull into the *Glowin' Galleon*, and Blossom leans forward to gawk at the full-scale neon pirate ship replica with LED rigging and neon painted sails. The place is loud and obnoxious and completely over the top.

"This is awesome," she mutters.

"You don't find it too much?"

"It's…" She stops gawking to meet my gaze. "Is it too much for you? Too many people?" A spark lights her brown eyes. "Let's sneak out. Everyone will wonder where we've gone."

I point to the group gathered at the entrance. "Except my family is already here." Mom waves. "And they've spotted us."

"And?" She shrugs. "We can still do a runner."

"I thought you wanted to be here?"

"Nerd boy, I want to be with you. Whether I'm kicking ass at paintball or putting together an elaborate prank, I just want to be with you."

My stomach dips at her words. She's serious. This gorgeous, outgoing creature wants to be with me.

I yank on her hand and she yelps as she falls over the console toward me. She's laughing when I capture her lips. I swoop my tongue inside and her laughter changes to a moan. She threads her hands through my hair and tugs as I deepen the kiss until—

Bang! Bang! Bang!

"Are you done making out?" Miles shouts. "We have a start time in fifteen minutes and we need to get kitted out."

I release Blossom's lips and lean my forehead against hers. "Your idea of doing a runner is becoming more attractive."

The door behind me flies open and I'm dragged from my seat out of the car by Miles. "Happy birthday!"

The rest of the Raider brothers pile on top of me until they're suffocating me. Blossom shoves them away.

"Your brothers are assholes," she mutters.

"This is not new information."

I dust off my clothes, and we walk hand in hand to the entrance where Mom and Stuart are waiting.

"How are you doing, daughter?" Mom asks as she engulfs Blossom in a hug.

"This marriage isn't real," Blossom says.

I frown. She was quick to point out our marriage is fake. Was I wrong about her? Does she not want to be with me? Does she not want me the way I want her? Am I merely a temporary fling to her?

"Sure, it isn't." Mom winks and Blossom blushes.

"Where are Dakota and Paisley?" Blossom asks.

"Paisley is not playing paintball when she's pregnant," Eli says.

"And Dakota is keeping Paisley company," Rhett adds.

Blossom snorts. "In other words, she's afraid to lose."

Kai rubs his hands together. "Them's fighting words."

"I bet I can win against you."

Kai extends his hand. "You're on. What do I get when I win?"

"I thought you preferred not to discuss hypotheticals that will never happen," Blossom says and Kai narrows his eyes on me.

"What have you been telling your girlfriend about me?"

I wrap an arm around Blossom. "Wife."

Blossom flashes her ring at my brother and the tension in my shoulders releases. Maybe she won't leave me after this marriage is annulled after all.

Mom sighs. "I'm loving this. Three of my boys are settled. Three more to go."

Stuart shakes his head. "Miles, Zane, and Kai aren't going to be as easy to settle as the others were."

"Easy?" Rhett mutters. "There was nothing easy about convincing Dakota to take a chance on me."

"Tell me about it." Blossom rolls her eyes. "I had to promise this one all kinds of sexual favors before he'd go out on a date with me."

"Sexual favors?" Mom asks and Blossom's eyes widen before she slaps a hand over her mouth.

"Shit. I didn't. Damn. I swore." She feigns zipping her lips. "No more talking from me."

I chuckle at how adorably embarrassed she is with her bright red cheeks.

I kiss her hair. "I'm still waiting on some of those sexual favors."

She slaps my shoulder. "You're supposed to pretend I didn't say anything embarrassing. Your research on how to woo a woman is a complete failure."

"As much fun as this is." Miles herds us toward the entrance. "I don't want to miss our time slot."

"In other words, he has a date later and is on a time schedule," Zane whisper-shouts to the rest of us.

"Time schedule?" Kai's nose wrinkles. "Why would you want to be on a time schedule?"

I moan. "Birthday rule. No complaining about time today."

Kai sticks his tongue out at me. "Fine. But I'll be thinking it."

"This is convenient," Blossom says as we enter the ship. "You can make up a rule for your birthday and it has to be followed?"

"Yep. And I have a few ideas for later."

Her eyes flare. "Tell me more."

"I'll tell you more." She leans close to me. "Tonight."

"Tease."

"This is not new information."

"We're in the Kraken's Hold arena," Miles announces and we follow him through the pirate ship to the changing room next to the arena where we don protective gear.

I'm happy for the protective gear when I stumble into the changing room thirty minutes later covered from head to toe in paint.

"I'm never celebrating my birthday with my brothers again," I grumble.

Blossom giggles when I pull my goggles up. I glance in the mirror. My entire face – except for where the goggles were – is covered in paint.

"Don't you start."

She holds up her hands. "You can't get mad at me. I defended you."

"Defended me? You barely got hit at all."

"But I never shot at you."

"Drinks are on Jaxon," Kai declares.

"Because he's the loser," Miles adds.

"Don't worry." Eli slaps my back as he passes me by. "I'm buying. I need to get Paisley. I'll meet you at the restaurant."

Blossom places a hand on her stomach. "I'm starving."

"Hurry up and change, sis," Zane says. "And we can eat."

Her smile lights up her face at the term 'sis'. "I love your family."

I nearly say I love her in return. But I don't. I can't possibly love her. It's too fast. Too soon. Except I've never felt this way about a woman before. Not even close.

My stomach knots like it's bracing for a hit. There's no universe where someone like Blossom – so warm, so alive – looks at someone like me and sees forever. I've been the odd one out my entire life. She's the kind of person who makes friends in line at the grocery store.

I need to be smart. Careful. Protect myself before I do something stupid.

I think of Dad at Eli's sixteenth birthday – smiling like nothing was wrong, playing Frisbee on the beach, making jokes. And then gone. No warning. No goodbye.

That's what love can do. Make you believe something that isn't real.

And Blossom… she still calls this marriage fake. Says it with a laugh, like it's all a game.

Maybe I need some space. Just enough to get my head on straight. To stop this thing from spiraling out of control.

Except – just the thought of staying away from her makes my chest ache. What if she doesn't notice I'm gone? What if it's easy for her?

That thought answers everything.

We're moving too fast. And I need to slow down. Before I forget, this was never supposed to be real in the first place.

Chapter 33

"Is this adulting? If so, I want nothing to do with it." ~ Blossom

BLOSSOM

I frown down at my phone. Jaxon hasn't returned a single one of my texts today. He's busy – he told me he had to work some late nights after his birthday – but, surely, he can take a moment to send a thumbs-up.

Dakota elbows me. "What's wrong?"

"Nothing."

She lifts an eyebrow. "You've been staring at your phone for five minutes with a scowl on your face for nothing?"

"Exactly." Time for a distraction. "Any news on becoming a foster parent?"

Since Dakota grew up in care, she wants to foster children who are in a similar situation as she was.

Paisley moans. "Fostering would be better than being pregnant."

"Are you having a lot of morning sickness?" I ask.

"No, I'm having a case of my husband becoming the pregnancy police. He's read one book on pregnancy and now he's an expert. He tried to correct the doctor at our last appointment."

The bell over the door dings as we enter *Pirates Pastries.* I inhale the scent of chocolate, cinnamon, sugar, coffee, and sigh. "I love this place."

"Me, too." Paisley narrows her eyes on me. "But if you tell Eli I was here, I'll fire you."

I roll my eyes. Since she's been pregnant, she's threatened to fire me on a daily basis. Don't tell so-and-so I'm here. Don't let so-and-so in while I'm working. Has she forgotten I've been her biggest defender since she hired me?

"What does Eli have against the bakery?" Dakota asks.

"I'm not allowed more than one coffee per day. And I should avoid too much sugar while I'm pregnant. You can't eliminate caffeine from a woman's diet and then tell her to avoid sugar. It's impossible."

"It'll all be worth it when your baby is here."

Parker enters the café from the kitchen. "It's the Raider women."

Paisley purses her lips as she pushes her glasses up. "My name is Bardot. I won't be changing it regardless of my martial status."

I gasp. "Did you get married to Eli without telling anyone?"

"I wish. Eli is planning an extravagant wedding."

"You're the one who fell in love with a billionaire," Dakota says.

"Don't remind me."

"What can I get you ladies today?" Parker motions to the display cases. "I have baked peaches and cream whiskey muffins, pirate's plunder muffins, shipwreck cookies, or Blackbeard's revenge cookies. I also have some new cookies for you to try. Kelpie crunch, Selkie bites, or Siren's snaps."

Paisley snorts. "You always did love your mythical sea creatures."

Parker narrows her eyes. "Are you saying Kelpie, Selkie, and Sirens don't exist?"

Paisley raises her hands. "I wouldn't dare. What's in a Kelpie crunch?"

"Sea salt and dark chocolate chips."

"I'll have a dozen."

"So much for avoiding sugar," I mutter.

"These cookies are for you to keep at your desk."

"Let me guess. They're for my boss."

Paisley grins. "I knew you were smart when I hired you."

Dakota and I quickly place our orders before we settle at a table near the window. I bounce in my seat.

"It's girls' day out. What do you want to do?"

Dakota groans. "If you say you want to go on an adventure, I'm going to hide in the bathroom until you leave."

I giggle. "You're silly. I wouldn't leave. I'd remove the door."

"I can't go on an adventure. Eli will have a heart attack."

I raise an eyebrow at Paisley. "And he won't have a heart attack when he finds out you're at *Pirates Pastries* having coffee and eating cookies?"

"Nope. Because I am accompanying my friends while I drink a green tea."

"You're such a liar," Dakota accuses.

"Fine." I huff. "We won't go on an adventure. What else can we do? There aren't any festivals happening this weekend."

Smuggler's Hideaway loves festivals. There's one practically every month. There's the Moonshine & Merriment Festival, the Mermaid Treasure Hunt, the Bootlegger Escape Room, Mermaid Lagoon Races, Smuggler's Reenactment Dinner, Hearts Beneath the Waves Festival, Find the Secrets of the Island Scavenger Hunt, and Ghost Tide Festival.

"You could always go to the Smuggler's Market," Parker suggests as she sets our drinks on the table.

The Smuggler's Market is a craft fair where locals sell quirky goods — such as bootleg jam, contraband candles, or smuggled sea salt caramels. It's nice, but it's not the adventure I was seeking.

I check my phone again. Still no message from Jaxon. I haven't heard from him in two days. If he hadn't told me he was going to be super busy working this week, I'd storm into his office the way I did the last time he ignored me.

Huh. Maybe I should storm into his office. The previous time had spectacular results after all.

Dakota snaps her fingers in front of my face. "Earth to Blossom. Earth to Blossom."

"I'm here."

"You're physically sitting here in this café but your mind is elsewhere." She wiggles her eyebrows. "Maybe on a certain nerdy Raider brother?"

Paisley studies me. "She always twirls a finger in her hair when she's thinking."

I drop my hand from where I was indeed twirling a finger in my hair. "I hate how observant you are."

"But you looooove Jaxon," Dakota sings.

I blow out a breath. "I do love the nerdy whiskey distiller."

But does he love me? He's ignoring me. Or am I being paranoid? I never suspected Alan cheated on me, but all I do is question Jaxon. It's not fair to him. I push all the worry out of my mind.

I will enjoy my day with my best friends and deal with Jaxon later. Tomorrow's Sunday after all. Surely, he won't work on Sunday.

Dakota cheers. "I'm so happy for you. We're going to be sisters. All three of us."

I hold up a hand. "Don't jump the gun. Jaxon and I haven't been dating very long."

"But you're married."

I frown. "You know why."

"I do know why. What I don't know is why you continue to wear his ring after your ex left the island."

I fiddle with the diamond. I hated how ostentatious this ring was when I first saw it. But now? Now I can't bear to remove it. I want the world to know I'm married to Jaxon. I want to shout from the rooftops how much I love him.

But since announcing my love for the nerdy distiller at Mermaid Karaoke would send Jaxon running to his lab never to return, I'll wear this ring and keep my mouth shut. Besides, Mermaid Karaoke season is over.

"I love sparkling," I claim.

Dakota doesn't appear to believe me but she doesn't have a chance to respond before the door bangs open and five men stumble into the bakery.

One of them notices us and makes his way toward us, banging into every table as he approaches. "Hey, pretty ladies."

I motion him away. "Go along now. Nothing to see here."

"As far as I'm concerned, lots of pretty to see here." He sways and I wonder if he's going to fall but he slams a hand on a table to keep himself upright. "Why aren't any of you dressed as mermaids?"

"We're not interested. Go back to your friends."

"I'm asking the redhead."

"She's pregnant. Let her be."

"What about you?"

I wave my hand at him. "Married and not willing to accept being second choice."

He points to Dakota. "What about you, doll? Third time's a charm."

"Is it?" She digs her phone out. "Let me ask my boyfriend."

One of his friends arrives and drags him away. "Sorry. He's drunk."

I stand and gather our things. "The Smuggler's Market it is."

"Good." Paisley grins. "I'm dying for a hamburger from *Salty Siren.*"

"Let me guess. Eli won't let you eat hamburgers either."

She sighs. "He read an article recommending pregnant women eat low-mercury fish to avoid possible adverse outcomes from the excessive consumption of red meat and now he believes red meat should be avoided entirely."

I thread my arm through hers. "Let's get you a big, juicy burger."

It's not exactly an adventure but at least I'm helping my friend covertly eat what she wants, despite what the father of her future child thinks. And it's taking my mind off Jaxon's inability to text me back.

Great. Now I'm thinking about him again. Ugh. This love stuff with Jaxon is more difficult than it ever was with Alan. Yet another piece of evidence proving I never loved my ex.

Chapter 34

"I don't understand what I did wrong." ~ Jaxon

JAXON

I ignore the beeping of my phone. It's been beeping on and off all day. Despite being holed up in my office working, I didn't switch off the sound. I couldn't. What if something happened to Blossom?

Blossom. My hands tremble as I reach for my phone. I haven't responded to her texts in two days. For all she knows, something bad has happened to me.

I am such an asshole. I open her latest message. It's a picture of her with Dakota and Paisley. She has her arms wrapped around her friends and her smile stretches from ear to ear.

My thumb hovers over the response button but I set the phone back down without responding. I won't engage. I need to stick to my resolution and keep my distance from Blossom before she breaks my heart.

The door handle jiggles. "Jaxon," Miles shouts as he knocks. "We know you're in there."

"I'm working!"

"Let me try," Zane says before the door handle jiggles again.

The door opens and Eli enters holding up a key.

I scowl at him. "Where did you get a key?"

"I have keys to every room in this building."

"But I had the lock added after the distillery was built."

Eli shrugs. "And your point is?"

I sigh. "Never mind. What are you doing here on a Saturday?"

"I think you mean, what are *we* doing here on a Saturday," Kai says. "Mr. Workaholic is nearly as bad as you."

"He doesn't spend as much time working since Paisley's pregnant," Miles says.

"He was here all day," Zane points out.

"What is everyone doing in my office?" I ask since this inane conversation can go on forever if I don't stop it.

Kai shrugs. "No idea. Big brother called us and ordered us to get our asses down here."

Eli sighs. "I didn't order you."

"You said you have good news. Same thing."

"What's the good news?" I could use some good news.

"I want to tell everyone at once."

The only person missing is Rhett. "We'll wait for Rhett."

"He's meeting us at *Rumrunner*."

"*Rumrunner?* Why didn't you say so?" Kai dashes out of the office without another word.

Miles grins. "Excellent. Another evening of watching Kai get rejected by Harper."

Zane rubs his hands together. "How many times do you think she'll reject him?"

The two saunter off discussing the odds.

"Close down. We'll follow them," Eli says.

I fiddle with my glasses. "Do I have to come? I'm busy."

"It's Saturday night. You shouldn't be working. I thought you'd relax more since you're dating Blossom."

Blossom. Why does every conversation lead back to her? Why can't I get her out of my mind? Or my heart?

"I'm in the middle of an experiment. I'll meet you there."

Eli crosses his arms over his chest. "This news involves you." He leans against my desk. "I'll wait while you finish."

Unfortunately, I lied. I'm not in the middle of an experiment. I switch off my computer.

"Let's get this over with."

We arrive at the speakeasy less than thirty minutes later. We join the rest of our brothers who are sitting at a booth near the stage where a band is setting up.

"What's this news?" I ask once I'm seated.

"Not everyone's here yet," Eli says.

"And we need to toast first." Kai grins as Harper arrives with a bottle of moonshine and shot glasses. "How are you, Harper?"

"I'd be better if I didn't have to stock shelves on a Saturday night."

"Can I help?" Kai stands but she glares at him.

"I think you've helped enough," she mutters before returning to the bar.

"Does that count as one rejection?" Miles asks and Kai hits him upside the head. "What? I was merely asking."

"We can't figure out who wins the bet without proper guidelines," Zane says and Kai growls at him.

Miles pours us shots of moonshine and passes them out. "Here's to the bootleggers. Masters of sneaky snips and secret stashes. Thanks for keeping the party alive."

"Thanks for keeping the party alive," my brothers repeat before downing their shots.

I sip on mine. Getting drunk when my brothers are around is a bad idea. Besides, I prefer to keep my wits about me. I have never enjoyed getting drunk and losing control of my thoughts. I like to keep control of my thoughts the same way I prefer my emotions to be steady and controllable.

"We're here," Rhett announces as he arrives at our table. I frown when I notice he isn't alone. Dakota, Paisley, and Blossom accompany him.

"What are they doing here?"

"Rude," Blossom mutters. Zane stands and offers her his chair. She smiles at him before sitting next to me. "Hey, nerd boy."

"Hello."

Her brow wrinkles. "What's wrong? You usually lose your mind when I refer to you as nerd boy." She waggles her eyebrows.

"Eli has important news."

She immediately sobers. "Is everything okay? Has something happened? Where are your parents? They're okay, aren't they?"

And now I feel like the biggest asshole in the world. Distancing myself from her doesn't mean I have to keep reminding her of her parents' death.

I want to reach for her to comfort her. But I don't dare. One touch and I'll be ensnared by her again. All my work of the past two days distancing myself will be for naught.

"I'm certain they're fine. They refuse to step foot in *Bootlegger* since the last time they were here Kai and Miles decided to strip down and streak through the bar."

She giggles. "Let me guess. It was a dare."

Eli knocks on the table to get everyone's attention. "I have news." His gaze settles on me. "Good news."

When he doesn't continue, Rhett growls. "Are we supposed to guess?"

Dakota pats his hand. "Don't be grumpy."

"What do you expect? I haven't seen you all day. I'm ready to whisk you home for some alone time."

Blossom sighs as she watches her friend. I want to reach for her but fist my hands instead.

"Tell them," Paisley urges. "Or I will."

"The way you told everyone you're pregnant before I wanted?"

"Your mom guessed."

"Fine." Eli meets Blossom's gaze and smiles. My stomach flips over and a growl builds in my throat as jealousy fills me. My brother shouldn't be smiling at my wife.

Blossom rubs my shoulder. "Be calm, nerd boy."

For a moment, I allow myself to enjoy the feel of this woman who makes me lose control of my emotions before pulling away. Her brow wrinkles.

"Alan dropped the lawsuit." Blossom gasps. "And he's paying you for your attorney costs."

"What? I don't understand. My lawyer didn't mention anything."

"I asked her not to."

Blossom blinks at Eli. "You asked her not to? Have you been in touch with my lawyer?"

"I had to contact her as she's the lawyer on record for the lawsuit."

"Eli," Blossom growls. "Please explain yourself. Because I know you couldn't have possibly taken over the defense of my lawsuit without asking me first."

"Told you so," Paisley whispers under her breath.

"I won't apologize."

Blossom's nostrils flare but Eli holds up a hand before she speaks.

"You obviously care about my brother. And he cares about you. I didn't want you to have this cloud hanging over your marriage. I'm sorry, Blossom. But I'm not sorry. I will always take care of my brother and the people he cares for."

Hanging over our marriage? Without Alan's lawsuit, there's no reason for us to be married.

"Can you arrange the annulment?" I ask Eli.

Blossom gasps. "Annulment? You want to annul our marriage?"

"It's what we agreed upon when we got married."

"When we got married?"

My brow furrows. "Yes, when we got married. Have you been drinking?"

She rears back. "Are you accusing me of being drunk?"

I push my glasses up my nose and she shoves a finger in my face. "No. You don't get to be all geeky and cute when we're having a serious discussion."

"I don't understand what's happening. We agreed to get an annulment when Alan dropped the lawsuit. Alan dropped the lawsuit. Thus, it's time to annul our marriage."

"Thus, it's time for us to annul our marriage," she mimics.

She jumps to her feet and the chair clatters to the floor behind her. "You're not socially awkward. You're an asshole." She rips the wedding ring off of her finger. "You don't want to be married. Here. Take your ring." She flings it at me. I try to catch it but it flies across the table and lands on the floor.

"And I haven't been drinking." She picks up the bottle of moonshine and pours the remaining liquid over my head. Once I'm completely wet, she slams the bottle down on the table. "Asshole," she yells and stomps off.

"I can't believe you. I thought you were the nice Raider brother." Dakota shakes her head before following Blossom.

Paisley sighs as she stands. "You've created a mess. And I'm not referring to your wet t-shirt."

Once she's gone, I ask my brothers. "What did I do wrong?"

Chapter 35

"And now you know why I don't trust men." ~
Blossom

Blossom

"Blossom!" Dakota chases after me and I hurry my pace.

Harper intercepts me. "Use the back hallway. There's an exit through the storage room no one knows about."

"You're a lifesaver."

She squeezes my hand. "I don't know what Jaxon did but you are strong. You'll be fine."

She's being sweet but I can't accept her kindness. I need to hold onto my anger a little bit longer. I can't fall apart in this bar in front of half of the island. Everyone will think I'm some silly girl. I'm not some silly girl.

I'm an idiot who was seduced by a triton. I never saw the male equivalent of a siren coming. I thought Jaxon was this nerdy man who has no social skills. Ha! He's an asshole who got what he wanted and now is done with me.

I should have figured it out when he refused to message me for the past two days, even though he knows how it causes me anxiety to be ignored.

I never should have lied to Alan. If I hadn't lied, I wouldn't have been forced to pretend Jaxon was my husband. And this whole charade wouldn't have happened.

No more should haves. I can't change the past. What's done is done.

"Thank you."

Harper nods before nudging me toward the back hallway. "Go. Dakota and Paisley are hot on your heels."

They are? I glance over my shoulder. Dakota and Paisley are pushing their way through the crowd. I don't wait. I run down the back hallway to the storage room and slam the door shut behind me.

Shit. It's dark in here. I search for the light switch but hit a bottle instead. It crashes to the floor. How am I going to find the secret exit in here?

"Blossom!" Dakota shouts as she bangs on the door. "We know you're in there."

I don't respond. She knows no such thing.

"I was born and raised in Smuggler's Hideaway," Paisley says. "I was sneaking out of the secret exit of Rumrunner before you knew the island existed."

"Thanks for reminding me of how much of an outsider I am."

The door flies open. I should have known a locked door wouldn't keep these two out.

With help from the light in the hallway, I watch Paisley and Dakota as they enter. Paisley doesn't hesitate. She marches straight to the light switch.

"Are you okay?" Dakota asks after Paisley shuts the door again.

"What do you think?"

She cringes. "Sorry. Stupid question."

"I'm confused." Paisley pushes her glasses up the nose and my stomach sinks as the gesture reminds me of Jaxon. "Did you or did you not agree to an annulment?"

"We agreed to an annulment before. When the marriage was fake. Before we started dating." My bottom lip trembles and my eyes feel hot, but I refuse to cry. Not yet. "I guess Jaxon always thought our relationship was fake."

Dakota grasps my hands. "No. That's not true."

"How do you know? Do you know he's been ghosting me for two days?"

"There could be a number of reasons for his failure to return your messages," Paisley says.

"Such as?"

"He got caught up in work. He dropped his phone in the toilet."

Dakota grunts. "That happened one time. Will you let it go already?"

Paisley's nose wrinkles. "You stuck your hand in dirty toilet water. No. I will not let it go."

While they argue, I scan the room. Where the hell is this secret exit? This place is a speakeasy but the speakeasy part is for tourists, right? There isn't seriously a secret exit left over from Prohibition in here?

"It's behind a fake wall," Paisley says.

"Can you show me where it is? I need to get out of here."

"I don't want you to be alone," Dakota says.

"I can't be in this bar. I can't be in the same building with the man I love who doesn't love me back." I sniff to stop the tears from falling. "Why didn't he pick me? No one picks me."

Dakota wraps her arms around me. "I'm sorry."

"Don't. Don't say you're sorry." After my parents died, all I heard was 'I'm sorry' over and over again. They're just words. They don't mean anything. They don't change anything.

"Okay. I'm not sorry. Jaxon is a complete asshole. Let's go get drunk and forget all about him."

I laugh as I pull away from her. "You don't drink, and she's pregnant."

"We can go to your apartment and eat tons of bad food and watch scary movies instead," Paisley suggests.

"It's a sweet suggestion, but I really want to be alone."

Paisley squeezes my hand. "But you're not alone. Whatever happens between you and Jaxon doesn't change a thing. You're still my friend."

"And mine," Dakota adds. "My best friend. You can't rescind best friend status. It's not allowed."

"Even if you refuse to go on a rollercoaster with me?"

She scowls. "I went on the rollercoaster."

"And peed your pants."

She huffs. "I did not pee my pants!"

"You two are sweet, and I love you to bits, but things are changing. You've got a little one on the way." I nod to Paisley's still flat stomach. "And you'll be busy with a dozen foster kids soon."

"I wouldn't say a dozen," Dakota mutters.

"And I'll be the best aunt I can possibly be."

But I won't be their sister. Once again, I'll be alone with no family. Silly me. I was so anxious to find a family, I didn't hesitate to embrace the idea of being a sister to the Raider brothers. I should have kept my heart encased in steel.

"I never should have married Jaxon."

"Your ex never should have sued you for half your inheritance," Paisley says.

"I really know how to pick men, don't I? Maybe I should join a convent. Do nuns brew beer? There are monks in Belgium who brew beer, why not nuns? I could open up a convent and start a brewery. I'm going to call it the brewing nuns. Would we get tax breaks for being a religious organization even though we brewed beer for profit?"

"Good question. Usually—"

Dakota holds up a hand to stop Paisley. "Are you seriously discussing opening a nun brewery right now?"

"I think the proper term would be convent brewery."

She moans. "I had to become best friends with two women who brew beer."

"Don't feel bad. I didn't give you a choice."

"Blossom!" Jaxon calls as he knocks on the door.

"Who told him where I am?" I whisper. "If Harper sold me out, I'm going to prank her so bad. She'll wish she never messed with a woman with a chemical engineering degree."

"I doubt Harper sold you out," Paisley whispers back. "Jaxon is an islander. He knows there's a secret entrance in here."

"And you didn't exit out the front door," Dakota adds. "Where else would you be?"

In the bathroom, crying my eyes out.

"Blossom! Can we talk?"

Is he kidding me? He wants to talk now? After he humiliated me in front of his entire family. Entire family? Scratch that. The entire bar? Hell. The entire island of Smuggler's Hideaway probably knows by now.

"Do you want to talk to him?" Paisley asks.

"No way."

She pats my shoulder. "I've got you." She walks to the opposite wall and pulls a bottle like a lever. The wall slides away, revealing a door.

I rush to it but pause with my hand on the handle. "Where will I go? He knows where I live."

"Go to Prohibition Beach. He'll never follow you there. It's where the family had Eli's birthday party before his dad left."

I feel a ping of sympathy for the fourteen-year-old boy who lost his dad. Losing your dad sucks. I know all about it. Except my dad didn't choose to leave me. He was taken from me. Having your dad choose to leave you must hurt worse.

I shove those thoughts away. I am not seriously standing here feeling sympathy for the man who threw me away without a second thought. We all have our histories, our issues, our trigger points. It doesn't give Jaxon an excuse to tell me we're getting our marriage annulled in front of his family.

I thought he chose me. I thought he wanted me. Wrong again.

"Blossom. Can we talk, please?" Jaxon asks through the door and spurs me into action.

"Prohibition Beach. Got it."

"Go. We'll keep him occupied. But I expect you to answer when I phone you later," Dakota says.

"I will." I always answer my phone.

My phone vibrates in my pocket. Correction. I always answer my phone unless an asshole is trying to reach me.

The door handle rattles and Paisley shoves me out the secret door before slamming it shut behind me.

I stumble outside and find myself in an alley.

"Hey!" A drunk couple stagger toward me. "Where's the speakeasy? We can't find it."

Tourists have to complete a riddle before the location of the speakeasy is revealed. One of the first things Paisley told me after she hired me was to never tell anyone where *Rumrunner* is. It's a Smuggler's Hideaway rule.

"Go right. It's the second alley."

"Thank you!"

They won't be thanking me when they end up in the alley behind Smuggler's Cove, where they keep their dumpsters.

I force a smile and make my way past them and toward the beach. Prohibition Beach is a small beach on the other side of the boardwalk.

Locals cast me sideways glances but I maintain a smile on my face until I reach the beach and ascertain it's empty. And then?

Well, then I let the dam break.

Chapter 36

"I should have learned to pick a lock when my brothers offered to teach me." ~ Jaxon

JAXON

"Are you seriously asking what you did wrong?" Eli asks.

"Even I know what you did wrong," Miles says.

I lift my glasses to massage the bridge of my nose. "Can we stop with the riddles? Just tell me what I did wrong."

"Dude." Miles shakes his head. "You hurt her."

My heart squeezes. I don't want Blossom to ever hurt. "It's probably for the better."

"Are you shitting me right now?" Rhett growls. "That woman loves you, and you love her. You need to fix this."

"But she left the minute things got tough." I shake my head. "She'll never stay with me."

Eli sighs. "I should have realized this."

My brow furrows. "Realized what?"

"You're afraid of being abandoned since Dad left us."

I scowl. "I am not afraid."

"Which is why you're sitting here discussing this with us instead of running after the woman you love."

I bristle. "I don't love Blossom."

"If you don't go after her now, she's never going to forgive you. You'll have lost her forever," Rhett says and my stomach drops to the floor.

I can't imagine a life without Blossom in it. Her smiles that light up a room, her goofy pranks, her ability to make friends with everyone she meets. She doesn't care how much of a nerd I am. She teases me about it until I kiss her. And then she explodes with passion.

It's a passion I want to experience every night for the rest of my life. While spending my days with her. Damn. Rhett's right. I do love her. And Eli's right, too. I was afraid she'd leave me.

So, I pushed her away. I ignored her for two days, knowing how much it hurt her. And then I declared my intention to get an annulment when what I actually want is to stay married to her until we're old and gray.

Eli grins. "He's getting it."

"What do I do?" I ask. "I can't lose her."

Kai shoves me out of my seat. "Go after her. Chase her. Show her you chose her."

I scan the bar. "Where did she go?"

I was asking my brothers, but practically everyone in the bar points to the rear hallway. I don't hesitate. The crowd parts for me as I run to the hallway.

The restrooms, Harper's office, and a storage room are here. I ignore the restrooms and the office. The storage room has a secret exit. I bet she's there. When I place my ear against the door, I hear muffled voices. Found you.

I knock. "Blossom! Can we talk?"

I wait a few moments but when she doesn't respond, I knock again. "Blossom. Can we talk, please?"

She still doesn't respond, so I try the door. It's locked. Should I ask one of my brothers to pick the lock? Before I can decide, I hear a shuffle. Shit. She's escaping through the back door.

I phone her, knowing she can't stand to ignore a call but I guess she can make an exception when it's me, since she doesn't answer.

I bang on the door. "Blossom!"

The door flies open but it's not Blossom. Dakota and Paisley glare at me.

"Where did she go? I need to make this right."

Dakota crosses her arms over her chest. "You hurt her. I don't care if you're my boyfriend's brother. I'm going to hurt you in return."

"I didn't mean to."

"Have you realized your mistakes?" Paisley asks, and I nod. "And you're ready to fight for her? She needs someone to fight for her."

"I'm ready." And I am ready. I was a fool who treated her poorly because I was afraid. I should have spoken to her and explained my fears.

"She's at Prohibition Beach."

"Prohibition Beach?" Shit. It's the beach we had Eli's six-teenth birthday party at before Dad left us. I never go there. I don't want the reminder. But losing Blossom is not an option.

Paisley squeezes my shoulder. "Fight for her, Jaxon. Show me I made the right decision in telling you where she is. Because she's going to give me a load of shit for it."

"I will." I motion to the secret exit. "Lock up after me?"

I don't wait for her agreement before rushing to the whiskey bottle and pulling it forward. There's a click before the fake wall moves out of the way to reveal the secret exit. I rush outside and down the alley.

People wave and greet me as I run to the boardwalk but I ignore them. I need to hurry. I have to get to Blossom.

When I reach Prohibition Beach, there's a lone figure hud-dled on the sand near the shore. "Blossom," I call as I approach.

She stands to face off with me. Her cheeks are stained with tears and her eyes are puffy and bloodshot from crying. Fuck. I did this to her. I hurt her.

"I'm sorry."

She leans her head back and shouts to the sky. "Enough with the sorry. It didn't mean anything when my parents died. It doesn't mean anything now."

"I shouldn't have said we can get an annulment in front of my family."

She scowls. "In front of your family?"

"I didn't mean to hurt you."

"You think you hurt me because you spoke in front of your family?" She shakes her head. "Leave. Just go."

"I'm not going anywhere until we figure this out."

"What is there to figure out? I love you, but you want an annulment. There's nothing to figure out."

My heart stops beating. "You love me?"

She rolls her eyes. "Duh. I realized I loved you when you went along with my crazy idea to prank your brothers. Although." Her nose wrinkles. "I knew I was falling in love with you before then. Probably from the moment you rushed me to the courthouse to marry me to stop Alan from stealing my money."

Warmth spreads through me at her words. All is not lost. I reach for her but she bats my hands away.

"Don't touch me, Jaxon."

I cringe at her use of my given name instead of her nickname for me.

"Petal—"

"Don't call me Petal. I'm not your petal. I'm not your anything. You want an annulment, remember?"

"I'm an idiot."

"If you expect me to disagree with you, you're going to be waiting a long time."

I'd smile at her sass, but I'm afraid she'll throw me in the ocean if I do.

"I don't expect you to agree with me. I expect you'll disagree with me often in the future."

She frowns. "Future. What future? We're getting an annulment, remember?"

"I don't want an annulment. I love you. I want you to be my wife."

Her mouth drops open. "You love me? You have a weird way of showing it."

This time, when I reach for her, she allows me to take her hands. "I love you but I was afraid."

"Of me?" She lifts her eyebrows. "I've never been accused of being scary before. Except for the time I dressed up as Jason, but it was Halloween and my friends dared me."

"I'm not afraid of you. I was afraid you'd leave me."

"Where was I..." She trails off and swears underneath her breath. "I'm an idiot. I should have realized."

I squeeze her hands. "How were you supposed to realize when I didn't?"

"Because I have more social skills than a sea cucumber."

I frown. "I have social skills."

"Jaxon, my nerd boy, I love you with all my heart, but social skills and personal awareness are not in your wheelhouse."

"You love me with all your heart?"

"I do. And I know you. It all makes sense now. Why you've never invited me to your house. Why you ignored me for the past two days. Why you asked for an annulment. You were afraid to fall too deeply in love with me because you have abandonment issues."

I clear my throat. "First of all, I never invited you to my house because I don't care about my house. It's a place I sleep. It's not my home."

"Good. Because I've driven by a few times and I am not a lover of split levels."

"And, secondly, I asked for an annulment because we agreed to get our marriage annulled after Alan dropped the lawsuit. We never discussed changing the agreement."

"Except we had sex and started dating and fell in love."

I frown. "I didn't want to assume."

"Let's make a deal."

"What kind of deal?" I ask with my heart in my throat. Is she going to break up with me? She said she loved me.

"Neither one of us will make assumptions about what the other is thinking or feeling from now on."

"I will agree to this deal if you'll put my ring back on your finger."

"You don't want an annulment?"

"Nope. I want you. I want to be married to the woman I love."

"We did things backward. We got married and then we fell in love."

I press a kiss to her lips. "I don't care."

She smiles and it warms my heart. I have her back, my Petal. She tugs her hand from mine and wiggles it at me.

"Ring, please. And then we can make out."

"I'm not having sex on this beach."

She smirks. "Famous last words."

Chapter 37

Harper – a woman who has no time or patience for a man-child

HARPER

I rub my back as I stretch forward to touch my toes. Saturday nights, when there isn't a festival in Smuggler's Hideaway, are usually quiet. Not quiet, as in dead. But quiet as in I normally don't have to kick anyone out.

But I'm sorely tempted to kick Jaxon Raider out. I don't know what he did but any man who gets a bottle of moonshine poured over his head by a woman probably deserves it.

And once news spread of the fight between Jaxon and his wife, Blossom, the nosy Nancies of Smuggler's Hideaway began appearing. At least they're ordering beer and food while they watch the show unfold.

Dakota and Paisley emerge from the rear hallway without Blossom. But Jaxon doesn't appear. I make my way to them.

"Please tell me Blossom and Jaxon used the secret exit and aren't making out in my storage room. I don't have time to get the ladder out to save a bra from the ceiling fan again."

Dakota giggles. "I want to hear that story."

"Trust me. The whole bar heard."

She grimaces. "Ew."

"Exactly."

"There's no need to worry," Paisley says. "They left through the secret exit."

Phew. "I never thought I'd be glad people know about the secret exit before."

She snorts. "As I recall, you knew about the secret exit before you started working here."

"Yeah, well, now I own the place and wish people would leave my storage room alone."

Kai sidles up to me, and I sigh. Here we go again.

"I'll help you clean up the storage room." He wags his eyebrows in case I didn't understand the blatant sexual innuendo.

I walk away without responding. Responding makes Kai think he has a chance. He doesn't.

"Burn!" Miles shouts.

"That's two rejections for tonight," Zane adds.

"I'm not certain the first one was a rejection."

"You think that because you want to win the bet."

A bet? The Raider Brothers are betting on how many times I'll reject Kai tonight? Typical. Those brothers have been a thorn in my side since Miles turned twenty-one. He thought he could sneak in his younger brothers. As if I didn't know the ages of everyone on the island.

The door opens and I sigh. We're nearing capacity tonight. And here I thought it was going to be a quiet Saturday. Nothing I can do about it now. Except warn my bouncer, Trent, about the capacity issue.

As I make my way across the bar, I nearly run into Blossom and Jaxon. They're holding hands and she's smiling from ear to ear. I guess they patched things up.

"I didn't expect to see you back here."

She rolls her eyes. "The Raider brothers were blowing up my phone."

Jaxon scowls. "I'll speak to them. They shouldn't take advantage of your inability to ignore your phone."

These two are adorable together. They were obviously meant for each other.

"I'm glad you worked things out."

Jaxon wraps an arm around Blossom and pulls her near. "I messed up but she forgave me."

"Lucky man."

"Yeah." He gazes at Blossom. "I am."

"Jaxon! Jaxon! Jaxon!" his brothers chant.

"You better get over there. The band will be pissed and not come back if the chanting gets louder than the music."

I'm lying. The band doesn't give a shit. But I love a family reunion.

I push my way through the crowd until I reach the bar. I maneuver behind it to the 'fancy' refrigerator. It's where I keep the stuff the regulars rarely order. I bend over and rummage through it until I find the bottle I'm searching for.

When I stand and whirl around, Kai is standing on the opposite side of the bar staring at me with heat in his blue eyes. I nearly shiver at the promise in those eyes.

I wait. I expect him to make some childish comment or over the top sexual innuendo. He doesn't. He smiles and waves before returning to the Raider table.

I don't have time to contemplate what that was all about. I grab nine champagne glasses before making my way through the crowd to Blossom and Jaxon.

"Congratulations," I say as I set the bottle on the table. "On the house."

Blossom jumps up from her chair to give me a hug. "Thank you. You're a sweetheart."

I chuckle. No one's called me a sweetheart before. Usually, it's ballbuster or bitch. Spoiler alert. I'm not a bitch because I dock your pay for showing up an hour late.

"I'm happy for you." I pull away and set the champagne glasses on the table.

"You're a secret romantic," Kai says and I scowl at him.

"What I am is none of your business."

"That's three!" Zane shouts.

"That is not three," Miles argues.

I glare at them. "You two are as immature as he is."

Miles smiles. "You say immature, I say youthful."

"I should have ratted you out to the police the first time you snuck your brothers in here."

Kai waggles his eyebrows. "You enjoy using handcuffs. Good to know."

Eli growls at him. "Enough. Harper has made it perfectly clear she wants nothing to do with you. Leave her alone. I taught you better than this. Respect the woman's choice."

I smile at him. "I always did like you."

Paisley sighs. "He is a pretty good guy." Eli swipes her glass of champagne and she growls at him. "Except when he's being the pregnancy police."

"You shouldn't have alcohol."

She snatches her glass back. "I'll have half a glass. Besides, there's no way we're toasting to me having another sister without champagne."

"You're stubborn."

"I'm right."

Jaxon pops the champagne bottle and everyone cheers. I start to back away.

"Stay," Kai says. "Join us for the toast."

"Sorry. There aren't enough glasses."

He dumps his beer into another glass. "I'll use this. You can have my glass."

I hold up a hand. "No, thank you."

"Come on. What's the big deal?"

"I don't want you to think you have a chance with me."

He bats his eyelashes. "I don't have a chance with you? Maybe a teeny tiny chance."

"Nope. Not even a teeny tiny, minuscule chance."

"Why not?" He scowls. "I'm a nice guy. I'm fun. I'm pretty good looking." He winks.

"You're a goofball who takes nothing seriously."

His nose wrinkles. "Where's the fun in being serious?"

And just like that. Any light-heartedness evaporates and anger ignites. "Life isn't fun. Life is hard work. Not all of us have billionaire brothers."

Eli raises his hands. "Leave me out of this."

"Sorry, Eli. But I can't. Not when you gave this man-child a job he can't handle."

"Hey!" Kai puffs out his chest. "I can handle my job just fine."

"Which is why my whiskey order from *Buccaneer's* was late this week and I had to stock the bar on a Saturday night when it's already busy."

"It was an oversight."

An oversight? He makes it sound as if he has no responsibility for the situation.

"This is why I will never give you a chance. You don't take anything seriously. I lost business this afternoon because I ran out of whiskey. And I sure as shit didn't run out because I made a mistake."

"I'm sorry."

I hold up my hand. "Don't apologize when you have no intention of rectifying the situation. It's a waste of my time."

I spin on my heel and stomp away. I can't believe I was ever tempted by Kai Raider. He's a child and a goofball. I don't have time for children or goofing around. I have this bar to manage. I don't have a family I can fall back on if I don't earn money.

Chapter 38

"I never thought I could be this happy." ~ Blossom

Blossom

"What do you think?" I ask as we park in front of the house.

Jaxon shrugs. "It's fine. All of the houses we've toured have been fine."

"I don't want fine. I want a forever home."

"Petal, are you putting too much pressure on this?"

"I haven't had a home since my parents died. I want a home," I insist.

"Okay." He kisses my cheek. "Let's go get you a home."

We get out of the car and walk hand in hand toward the house. I love it already. It has a wraparound porch. I can imagine us sitting on the swing sipping whiskey or beer and watching the sun set.

The door opens and our realtor, Jade, steps outside.

"First impressions?" she asks.

I smile. "I love the bright red door and black siding."

She motions us into the house. I bite my tongue before my jaw drops to the floor. The entire first floor is an open concept, allowing a view of the ocean through the French doors to the deck.

"Sold," Jaxon says.

"What?"

"It has a front porch you love, a view of the ocean, and I spotted a hot tub on the deck."

"We haven't seen the rest of the house."

"As long as it has good bones, we can fix it up however we want."

"We don't know how much it costs."

Jade clears her throat. "It's at the top of your budget at five hundred thousand."

"It's a seller's market. How much do we need to bid to get this house?" I ask.

"I'll cover the extra cost."

I glare at Jaxon. "We agreed to split the cost of the house fifty-fifty."

"I'm not letting you spend all of your inheritance on a house."

Jade groans. "I'll be outside on the deck."

I wait until she shuts the door behind her before laying into Jaxon.

"You don't let me do things. I do what I want."

He sighs. "Please excuse my terminology. I don't want you to spend all of your inheritance on the house."

I cross my arms over my chest. "Better. And?"

"And I shouldn't have spoken about money in front of the realtor?"

I kiss his cheek. "Good job."

"I'm confused. Does this mean we're buying the house and I'm paying the extra cost?"

"Nope." I shake my head. "We're still splitting the cost fifty-fifty."

"What about keeping your inheritance money to pay for college for our kids?"

My heart thumps in my chest. "Kids? We never discussed having children."

"Oh. Do you not want children?"

He appears adorably confused. I debate allowing him to be confused a little longer but I can't. After our big blowout, we agreed to be honest with each other at all times.

"I do want children."

"As do I."

"How many do you want?"

He shrugs. "How many bedrooms does this house have?"

I giggle. "Are you seriously deciding how many children we should have based on the size of this house?"

"You love this house. You spent an hour last night in bed staring at the pictures."

"I thought you were asleep."

Jade enters the house again. "I figured it was safe to return since you aren't yelling at each other and there's no broken glass."

"How many bedrooms does this house have?" Jaxon asks.

I let Jade answer despite knowing everything there is to know about this house. I did spend an hour last night staring at pictures online. "Five but you may want to use the small bedroom as an office."

"Four bedrooms minus the primary suite means three children. Do you want to give me three children?"

Warmth spreads through me. Jaxon may have stumbled but ever since we talked things out on the beach, he's been one hundred percent in this relationship. We haven't spent a night apart and he always answers his phone when I call. He's the perfect partner. I never thought I could be this happy.

"I'll give you as many children as you want." It's the truth. Whatever Jaxon wants, I'll give him.

He frowns. "That's my line."

I wrap my arms around his neck and kiss him. "Let's not make any decisions about children today."

"Okay. We can always buy another house if we decide to have more."

"There's already planning permission to add a mother-in-law suite," Jade says.

Jaxon's brow wrinkles. "I don't have a mother-in-law."

"She means we could add another bedroom and bathroom. Am I right?" I ask Jade.

"Correct. The addition would be on the ground floor. You could move your primary bedroom downstairs with the children upstairs."

I giggle. "Leave Raider children alone? Not a good idea."

"Maybe Nelson-Raider children will behave," Jaxon says and my eyes get hot.

"Nelson-Raider?"

"You don't have any siblings and your parents are gone. I thought you might want our children to carry your name."

I sniff but I can't stop the tears from falling.

"What did I say wrong?" Jaxon wipes the tears away. "Tell me how to fix this."

"You know the rule. Hold me until the tears stop."

He tightens his arms around me. "Please, don't cry. I can't bear it when you're sad."

"I'm not sad. I'm moved by how sweet you are. By how much you understand me."

"I love you, Petal." He kisses my hair. "I know you better than anyone else."

I lean back to meet his gaze. "Better than I know myself?"

"Um…"

"Why don't I show you the upstairs bedrooms before you decide to make those babies now?" Jade asks.

Jaxon's cock twitches against my stomach. I guess I don't need to ask if he's ready to make babies with me.

"Go." He kisses my nose. "I need to grab something from the car."

"What do you need to grab?"

"You'll see."

"You're being mysterious."

"Good." He smiles and kisses my nose before releasing me and heading outside.

Jade sighs when he's gone. "Girl, I don't know how you did it but you have that man wrapped around your finger."

"Good. Since I'm wrapped around his."

"I'm happy for you."

I squeeze her shoulder. "You'll find your happy-ever-after someday."

She rolls her eyes. "I've dated every man on this island who is age appropriate and some who weren't. I think I'm done."

"You never know what the future will bring."

"I do. The future will bring us upstairs to view the bedrooms."

I follow her up the stairs and quickly tour the five bedrooms. Besides the one small bedroom, they're all a good size. Plus, there are three bathrooms. Two bedrooms have attached bathrooms while the remaining two bedrooms share a Jack and Jill bathroom.

"It's perfect," I tell Jade as we walk down the stairs where Jaxon is waiting for us in the kitchen.

"You want to put in an offer?"

I glance at Jaxon. "Asking price plus ten percent to start," he says.

"I'll make up the offer and let you know how the buyers respond. Lock up when you leave." Jade waves as she shuts the door behind her.

I make my way to Jaxon and he pulls me into his arms. "Do you want to tour the upstairs bedrooms?"

"Later. First, I have a surprise for you."

"A surprise? We just bought a house. Isn't that enough of a surprise?"

He hands me a gift bag. "I enjoy surprising you."

"What is it, nerd boy?"

He growls. "Do not get me all horny. I am not having sex in this house until we own it."

I waggle my eyebrows. "But once we do, we'll have sex in every room?"

"As often as you wish." He presses his lips to mine but when I try to deepen the kiss, he retreats.

"Open your present."

I remove a bottle of whiskey from the bag and read the label. "Cherry Tidings."

"It's the holiday whiskey I was working on when you inspired me to add the cherry flavor."

"You named it after me?"

He brushes the hair off my forehead. "Of course, I did. Without your inspiration, this whiskey wouldn't exist."

"You're really killing it at being the best boyfriend ever."

"Husband," he corrects.

"I love you, husband of mine."

"And I love you, Petal."

I never thought lying to my ex to stop him from stealing from me would lead me to love, but here I am. Standing in my new house, I plan to make a home with the man I love.

His phone beeps with a message. "It's not you. I'll ignore it."

But then my phone beeps with a message. "Go ahead. I know you have to answer."

I've been going to therapy to deal with the trauma of losing my parents and the aftermath with Alan, but I haven't managed to 'cure' my impulse to answer every message and every call yet.

I dig my phone out of my pocket and open the message. I gasp when I read it.

"What? What's wrong?"

"Nothing's wrong. It's a message from Jade. We got the house."

"We got the house?"

I nod.

He smirks. "Excellent. Time to begin our journey of having sex in every room."

"You won't hear me say no."

"Love you, Petal," he mutters before his lips crash to mine.

Chapter 39

About the Author

D.E. HAGGERTY IS AN American who has spent the majority of her adult life abroad. She has lived in Istanbul, various places throughout Germany, and currently finds herself in The Hague. She has been a military policewoman, a lawyer, a B&B owner/operator and now a writer.

Printed in Dunstable, United Kingdom